TRYING TO WIN AT LOVE

A journey through an extraordinary USTA tennis season

By Eric Lee

Author of
Murder in a Country Town and other stories
Murder in a Coastal Town and other stories
Murder in a Snow Covered Town and other stories
Trying to Win at Love Again

Paragon Publishing
Professional Fiction Publisher
El Sobrante, California, USA

Author website: www.ericleestories.com

For information address:

 Paragon Publishing
Professional Fiction Publisher
2300 Greenridge Drive
El Sobrante, California, 94803

Author website: www.ericleestories.com

Substantial discounts on bulk quantities of this author's publications are available to corporations, educational disciplines, professional associations, and other qualified organizations. For details and specific discount information, visit ericleestories.com and click on the "Contact Us" link at the bottom of the website. For more information about the author's stories, visit ericleestories.com

Printed in the United States of America

Trying to Win at Love
    Eric Lee
    Library of Congress Catalog-In-Publication Data
    ISBN: 978-0-9674476-5-0

Table of Contents

Acknowledgements

I acknowledge that the sky is blue, fire is hot, and life is short. I also acknowledge that my opponents in tennis rarely think the lines are "in" on match point. Most of all, I acknowledge that without the help of so many friends and family, this book would not have been possible.

After publishing three mystery and suspense short story collections, my friend Bill Raynolds challenged me to write in a completely different genre. I decided to tell a story about my passion, tennis. No sport combines athleticism, aggression, precision, strategy, and teamwork quite like tennis. The lessons that I have learned on the court have been instrumental in shaping my life off the court.

There are too many people to thank in this small space, but I would like to acknowledge the following people who went above and beyond the call of duty to help me put this book together:

Matt Clark
Brenda Douville
Ellen Hanscom
Gary Kurtzman
Clarence Lee
Gloria Lee
Damon Maxey
Ross Parker
Bill Raynolds
Pat Sutton

Preseason and Taking the Reins

"Hi Dale," I said. I always enjoyed chatting with Dale, my captain and tennis mentor ever since I joined the USTA. Now in his late sixties, Dale's hair is grayer and his court coverage more limited. But, his mind is as sharp as ever. "Ready to repeat as league champions?" I asked.

"That's what I wanted to talk to you about," Dale said, pausing to lightly chuckle. "I just got the word that I've been moved from a 4.0 rating level down to 3.5. So, I was hoping you'd take over as captain of the 4.0 team."

"Me? Captain? Nah, I wouldn't want to do that."

"Come on, you're friends with the guys. The team is already set up. All you need to do is determine the weekly lineups and organize practices."

"No thanks. I don't want to decide who plays and who doesn't." There was another reason I didn't want to be the captain, but I didn't want to say it to Dale. I've had high blood pressure for years and have fought to keep it under control without medication. I feared what the stress of captaining a competitive team would do to my health.

"You're the best option. I know it. Won't you just think about it?"

"Hold on." I raised my finger in the air and paused momentarily. "Okay, I thought about it. Find someone else."

"Alright, let me make some calls. We'll talk again this weekend."

I didn't really think about my conversation with Dale again until the weekend. He had called me to complete a foursome for doubles tennis. Dale knew I was a tennis-aholic, ready to play at a drop of a hat. Two other long-time members of the Albany team, Barry and Lloyd, joined us.

Barry and Lloyd are proven leaders, on and off court. Each have been successful USTA captains and business entrepreneurs. Barry, married with no kids, owned and operated his own auto repair shop for many years. With graying facial hair and a happy-go-lucky personality, Barry reminded me of a thin Santa Claus. Lloyd, who is married with an adult son, recently formed his own real estate business. Lloyd, a little shorter and stockier than Barry, had a brilliant mind, regularly thinking three steps ahead of everyone else.

As we stretched on the sideline, Dale said, "Guess what. I found the perfect captain for the 4.0 tennis team."

"You have?" I said, wondering whether it would be Barry or Lloyd. "Who?"

"You," Dale said.

"What? We've discussed this. I'm not interested."

"Yes, but I've got you some help. Barry has agreed to be your co-captain and Lloyd will help if you need to make any tough decisions." Barry and Lloyd, both in their fifties, nodded in agreement.

"Hold on a minute," I said, realizing this wasn't really a planned tennis match, but a carefully organized intervention. "I've never been a captain before. Why can't one of you two do it?"

Lloyd cited his new real estate business while Barry used a European vacation during the playoffs as his alibi.

Although it sounded great that Barry would be a co-captain, I knew better. As Dale's co-captain for three years, I knew that all of the responsibility and potential player frustration lies with the captain. "Like I told Dale, I have a bunch of good friends on this team. Every captain makes decisions that people don't like, and I don't want to be put in that position."

"You don't get it," Dale said. "It's because you have this great relationship with the players that you're the right man for the job."

I shook my head. "You have to find someone else."

"There is no one else," Dale said. "I've been asking all week. Today's the deadline for all captains to register their teams. If you don't do it, there will be no Albany team."

"Really?" I said, surprised.

"Really," Dale said, nodding. "The team would be split up. Some guys might not be able to find another team."

I ran my hand through my hair in frustration. I paused to ponder which was the bigger negative: captaining the team or not having a team. "Okay," I finally said. "I'll do it."

That Sunday night, after registering the Albany 4.0 team, I read a portion of the "newbie" captain's manual on my home computer. Then, I researched online the other nine registered teams in our league.

"Eric!" my girlfriend Stacey shouted from downstairs. In a word, I'd describe her as "hot" and in two words, "really hot". I could gaze at her flowing black hair, tan skin, and perfect smile all day. Like me, Stacey is 36 years old. We've been in a committed relationship for the last two and a half years, which means everyone and their mother (especially mine) wonders when we are getting married. Lately, Stacey has been dropping not-so-subtle hints about marriage and her biological clock. She has been a successful lawyer for the last ten years, but I get the strong feeling that she wants to settle down and have a family. For now, I'm content with the current arrangement, which includes her coming over to my house to spend Sunday evenings together. "What are you doing up there?! Dinner's ready."

"Coming!" I shouted as I studied San Leandro's and Union City's rosters. I expected they would be the top two teams in the league. Last year, we finished fourth in our league and upset the #1 seeded team, San Leandro, team in the first round. Because our league had a wild card, we and #2 seed Union City advanced to Districts.

"You're on the USTA website," Stacey said, now right behind me. She had snuck upstairs and began peering at the computer screen. "I thought you were doing work."

"Well," I said, spinning my chair around toward her. "It is work, sort of. I just agreed to captain the tennis team this year."

"What? Why? Isn't that's going to take a lot of your free time?"

"No, it won't. It'll just be filling out lineups and organizing practices," I said, parroting Dale's claim.

"Yeah, right. Tell that to someone who doesn't know you. Whenever you agree to do something, you're fully invested. There's no halfway with you. You'll never keep it to just lineups and practices."

"You don't know that."

"I do," Stacey said, sitting on my lap. "You've been up here for the last 30 minutes." She leaned close to me. "Are you organizing a practice? Filling out a lineup?"

I looked at Stacey and couldn't help but smile. It was scary how well she knew me. "Guilty as charged, counselor," I said before closing my laptop and kissing her on the lips. "Okay, let's eat."

After dinner, my dad called me from Los Angeles. My dad, whom I have looked up to my entire life, taught me the game of tennis as a youngster. He played tennis tournaments as a young adult, but quit competitive tennis when winning began to take precedence over the fun of the game. Because tennis had been such a big part of his life, I have always longed for him to be proud of any of my tennis achievements.

My dad lives by two basic rules. In life, you have to pick your battles and when you do, don't look outward for validation of your efforts. In essence, don't let others define your success. As an example, when my parents applied to get me into a private junior high school, I had to undergo many hours of interview preparation. Exasperated, I said to my dad, "I've had enough. If I don't get in, it just means that I'm not smart."

He looked at me and said, "No. If you don't get in, it just means they're not smart." Ever since, his words and actions have always had a profound effect on me. Yet, here I found myself excited to tell him that I'm the new Albany captain as if I were looking to him for validation.

"Why did you agree to take on the role of captain?" my dad asked over the phone. My heart dropped. Rather than hearing "congratulations" or "what a great thing to do", I would be listening to a lecture. My dad didn't wait for me to answer his question. "You just finished a busy tax season where you worked 60-hour weeks. Now, during your offseason, you want to go through the stress of being the captain." Like me, my dad has high blood pressure, and he routinely lectures me on eating right and watching my stress level.

I remained silent, knowing his lectures end quicker if I don't interrupt. I know his comments come from a genuine place of concern. Two years ago, my dad fainted shortly after returning home from a morning jog and it gave the whole family a scare.

"You don't think this will aggravate your blood pressure?" he asked.

"It could, but I won't let it. I can control how I deal with the stress."

I could hear my dad tapping his fingers as I patiently waited through the silence. He finally spoke, "Just promise your father you'll get a physical in the next few weeks to make sure you're healthy."

"I promise," I said.

I must admit that my dad and Stacey were right. As captain for just a day, I already cared more than ever about the success of the team. As a small, public court team, Albany has always been at a huge disadvantage. We didn't have the luxury of a tennis club or large public facility to recruit team members. Although our Albany players were far from poor, the club teams in our league hailed from more affluent neighborhoods and their players poured far more money into improving their tennis game, everything from expensive rackets to lessons from club pros. Despite these inherent limitations, the Albany men's team, led by Dale, won seven straight league championships, making him a living legend around the Albany courts. Dale's seven championships included six at the 3.5 rating level and then last year as the new kids on the 4.0 rating block. So, how did we beat the odds to be so successful in the past?

Dale was able to recruit a small group of loyal, committed players who made USTA league tennis a top priority in their life. They planned their schedules around games and practices. They diligently worked to improve their game. Over the years, this committed group of players became a family. In the end, that's why I became captain. I couldn't bear to see this family broken up.

With Dale's departure, I knew how important it was to ensure that each player knew our Albany team would still be intact. As soon as Dale announced the leadership change over email on Monday, I started to call teammates to personally tell them about my promotion to captain, and see if they were ready to go for this season.

I started with Doug, our best player. In his mid-fifties, he found the fountain of youth last year, regularly beating opponents half his age in singles. I looked forward to building my team around Doug, a smart, crafty player who simply wears down his opponents.

Hey, Doug, my #1 singles player. I'm going to be captain of the 4.0 team and I was wondering...

I'm 4.5 now.

Come again?

I've been moved up. My rating level is now 4.5. I can't play on a 4.0 team. Didn't Dale tell you?

No, no. He conveniently left that out. [I muttered under my breath incoherently.]

Uh, anything else? We were just sitting down for dinner.

Well, have you thought about appealing your rating? I mean, I've seen your backhand and, well, it could use some work.

What? You're saying my backhand is weak.

Well, for a 4.5, yeah. But hey, it's better than mine.

Thanks for the backhanded compliment.

[I laughed, adding extra chuckles hoping he would appreciate it.] So, uh...

I'm not appealing my rating.

Okay, enjoy your dinner.

I slowly drew a line through Doug's name and stared at the roster. I decided to call Nelson, our #2 singles player from last year and, since ten seconds ago, our best singles player. I double-checked his rating on the USTA website. Thankfully, he was still a 4.0.

Hi, Nelson. Just wanted to make sure you're going to play with us this year.

I'd love to, but I got a new job.

That's not a problem. You don't have to play in every match.

You don't understand. The new job is in Dallas. [Long pause.] Eric, you still there?

Barely. Um, when do you leave?

Next week. [Another long pause.] Eric?

Yeah, sorry. I guess, um, have a safe trip.

Now, I had no choice but to call Billy, the youngest member of the team. Some might consider him high maintenance. He doesn't have a car, so the captain has to pick him up and take him to road matches. Then, navigating his studying and full personal life with the league schedule is also a challenge. If you're the captain, you ask yourself, "Why is Billy on the team? He's great, but is he really worth the trouble?" Last year, Dale decided that he wasn't, rarely playing him in our playoff run. However, with the loss of Doug and Nelson, I needed Billy... badly. Besides, I liked and admired Billy, mostly because he has overcome such adversity. He lost his father to a car accident in his early teens and is now paying his own way through his senior year of college with scholarships and band gigs. He has a never quit attitude, both on and off the court. Although short in stature at five foot six, he's long on grit and determination, reminding me of a mini Rafael Nadal.

Hi, Billy. I will be taking over as captain of the Albany team. Just wanted to see if my #1 singles player was ready to go.

Yeah, but I'm in a band and we play on weekends. So, can you make the matches on weeknights after 7:00 PM?

Billy, you know our home courts don't have lights.
Okay, I can swing it to make Saturday matches at 10:00 AM.
Can you make the home matches at that time?
I don't know. I can't schedule all home matches based on one player's availability.
I'm taking an advanced tennis class as an elective this semester. My coach says I now have a 5.0 forehand.
Saturday mornings it is.

Next, I called Ross, our top doubles player and most athletic player on the team. Extremely competitive, Ross starred on his high school baseball, basketball, football, and tennis teams. In excellent shape, his leaping ability and endless energy frustrates his opposition. At age 30, he is still on a high school campus as a history teacher, and he loves it. Clean cut and with a conservative appearance, Ross is the picture of the All American boy. Married with two young boys and a recently purchased fixer-upper home, Ross might not have much time for tennis this year.

Hi, Ross. Just calling about the upcoming USTA league. I'm hoping you're going to play…
Yeah, I'm in. In fact, I have a buddy. His name is Chris. He just moved back into this area. I want to play doubles with him this year. Can he join the team?
Hmm… tell me about his game.
Chris is thirty years old…in excellent shape.
How's his tennis game?
Oh, he has excellent range. A natural athlete. He played varsity basketball and baseball with me in high school.
How about tennis? Has he ever played tennis?
I've actually never seen him play, but he's a great guy.
[To a captain, hearing a prospective player is a great guy is like hearing your blind date has an excellent personality. It's

15

true that it helps, but it's not what you really want. Now that I'm captain, I'll take a convicted felon with a good serve and volley game. I began to worry that Chris might weigh down Ross. However, I couldn't afford to upset my best doubles player. As I pondered these thoughts, I heard Ross yelling in my ear.]

Eric! Are you there? Eric!

Yeah, sorry. What were we talking about? [I hoped Ross may have forgotten.]

So, can Chris join the team? [Darn it. He hadn't.]

Yeah, have him come out to practice.

Next, I called Peter, the player I wanted to team up with Ross. Peter, an intense competitor, had a vicious left handed slice serve and two-handed backhand that would make Jimmy Connors proud.

Hi, Peter. Ready to play some league tennis this year?

Maybe in a wheelchair league.

What?

You didn't hear? I tore the ACL in my knee about a month ago. I'm out at least 9 months. It makes me sick.

That makes two of us.

I'll try to come out and cheer you guys on. Maybe in the playoffs.

What playoffs?

Huh?

Never mind. Take care of yourself.

As I scanned the roster, I knew who I wanted to call next. I needed cheering up. One of the nicest guys on the team is Doc, who actually is a doctor. In baseball terms, Doc is what you call an "innings eater", available for almost every match and is happy to play. In his mid-fifties and wearing eye-glasses, Doc looked more like a geek than an athlete. Tall and lanky, Doc is a smart, steady player that routinely frustrates younger opponents. As a former long distant runner, he had the best conditioning and stamina on the team. His greatest attribute though is his wife, who makes the best homemade appetizers for our home matches.

Hi, Doc. Just checking to see if you're ready to play 4.0 adult tennis.

Yeah, I retired from my job five months ago, and have been playing tennis three times a week. My game has really improved. How's the team looking?

A lot better after hearing that.

I was hoping to play mostly singles this year. Is that okay?

Yeah, that's fine. You'll be my #1 singles player. [Man, I hope these guys never talk to each other about my conversations.]

Sounds great. I'll sign up for the team tonight.

After calling everyone on the team, I began studying the roster. Of the eight guys that won the local league championship for us last year, five have been moved up to 4.5, one moved to Dallas, and one has a season-long injury. Only Ross would be returning and he wants to partner with a guy who may or may not have touched a tennis racket before. It looked like this was going to be what the pros call a "rebuilding year" for our 4.0 team.

The USTA has an official description of rating levels which range from 2.5 to 5.5 for adult league play. My completely unofficial description, in layman's terms, of each rating is as follows:

2.5 – Let's face it. You stink. You're pretty sure how to score. The good news is that you never forget your score since it rarely changes. The service box seems awfully tiny to you.

Forehand usually goes in the direction of the net and backhand… well, what backhand?

3.0 – You still stink. You're now able to break serve even when your opponent doesn't double fault four times in a row. Forehand not only goes in the direction of the net, but over it every now and then. Your backhand still sucks, but you figured out how to run around it as much as possible.

3.5 – You have read some tennis self-help books, practiced diligently, taken a few tennis lessons, and, surprise, surprise, you still stink. On the positive side, your first serve is now a weapon, even if it is so wild you might hit the back fence on the fly. Even though you're no longer allergic to the net, you still choke on half your overheads.

4.0 – You have all the strokes with none of the consistency. Some days you think you can't be beat and other days, even extra deodorant cannot stop you from stinking.

4.5 – You think you have turned the corner. You have a powerful first serve and a kick second serve. Your forehand is a lethal weapon and backhand is great. You're proud of your repertoire of lobs, drop shots, and passing shots. Your entire game smells like a rose and you feel you're ready to compete at the 5.0 level.

5.0 – You're good enough to beat a cocky 4.5 player 6-0, 6-0 and tell him he stinks.

5.5 – You've reached the mountain top where the air is fresh and no one stinks… unless a tennis pro is smelling.

My rating scale demonstrates a simple USTA league truth: tennis ability is all relative. You can't get too down or too high about your tennis ability because there is always a player out there that can make you look like a star or humble you so much you consider throwing your gear in a nearby lake.

About a week after becoming captain, I began to wonder if I made the right decision. The reality was I didn't pursue this position. I didn't even want it. More importantly, I had no idea whether the players wanted *me* as their captain. These players, half of them my elders, are lawyers, businessmen, policemen, teachers, and other leaders in their respective professions. I wondered whether they'd respect me as their leader.

"What's wrong?" Stacey asked, looking me straight in the eye across the dinner table.

"What makes you think something is wrong?" I asked, beginning to re-orient myself.

"You've been quietly playing with your salad for the last minute. You do that when something is bothering you."

"I'm just worried about taking over as captain. I want the team to do well and for people to respect me as a leader."

"They liked you as a teammate, right?" Stacey asked. I nodded. "Then, they'll like you as a captain. You worry too much."

I looked at her, slightly amazed. "You make it sound so simple."

"It *is* simple." She pointed at me. "You make it complicated."

I smiled before eating my salad.

About a week later, we had our first team practice. We have a very close-knit team, and although practice can feature some fierce competition, it is always fun and lively. I scheduled the practice Saturday morning so Billy could make it. When he arrived, someone shouted his nickname, "It's The Kid!" in the same way the entire bar shouted out "Norm!" in the television show *Cheers*. It's funny how nicknames start. First, people called him "Billy", then it switched to "Billy the Kid" and now they've dropped his first name altogether. The Kid, whose curly, black hair grew wildly underneath his baseball cap, had a boyish face which displayed dimples when he smiled. He held up his right arm and grinned as if he was acknowledging a large crowd chanting his name.

Craig, one of our singles players, arrived next. Despite a divorce and child care issues with his pre-teen son, he made USTA league tennis a priority in his life. Craig wears the same buzz cut that he had years earlier as a US Marine. He embodies Mark Twain's old quote, "It's not the size of the dog in the fight. It's the size of the fight in the dog." The shortest member on our team, Craig was the toughest, most intense competitor. I've seen him prevail on a sheer will to win and a stubbornness to not give in to losing. Now a partner in his law firm, the forty year old Craig had taken a mentor role to Billy, who had planned to go to law school in the Fall.

"So, what are your plans for this summer?" I overheard Craig ask Billy as they stretched.

"I'm going to get a summer job to supplement my income from the band gigs."

"How'd you like a summer internship at my law firm?" Craig asked. "You'd have to go through the interview process, of course, but the internship would be a great experience for you."

Billy's eyes lit up. "Yeah, that would be cool."

Craig tapped the bill of Billy's cap and said, "You'll just need to get a haircut." Billy and I laughed before Craig added, "I'll email you more about the internship on Monday."

Once ten players arrived at practice, I asked everyone to gather around.

"Oh no, not a team meeting," Mike complained good-naturedly. Mike, a team elder, is quite the jokester. His favorite form of exercise is running his mouth, but it's people like Mike that remind me that the point of the league is to have fun. A long time high school English teacher, Mike may have missed his true calling as a stand-up comedian. Sporting a full head of sandy blond hair, Mike acted and looked years younger than his actual age. A fitness fanatic, Mike wakes up at 5:30 AM every morning to work out at the gym.

"It'll be quick. A five minute meeting," I said to Mike, who immediately looked at his watch. Probably due to my training as a CPA, I like things organized and structured. Unfortunately, most of the team feels organization and structure is what their work and family life is for.

I introduced newcomer Chris, Ross' friend, who awkwardly waved to the group. Chris' boyish, clean-shaven face made him look younger than thirty years old. Chris looked like a blond hair, blue eyed Abercrombie & Fitch model. With broad shoulders and strong build, he had the physical attributes of a perfect athlete.

I then discussed everyone's least favorite topic, team dues: $20 per person to cover the home court reservations and game balls. After some groaning from a group that included doctors, lawyers and successful businessmen, most of the guys paid me.

"I just want to say something," Lloyd said to the group. "We came dangerously close to not having a team this year, but Eric stepped up to save the squad by taking over as captain. Let's hear it for Eric." The group chanted my name and gave a light applause. It felt good to get the appreciation of my teammates.

"Thank you," I said, holding my hand up. "Okay, let's play some tennis."

On court #1, I had Mike and Al play Ross and Chris. I thought this would be an interesting matchup. Mike is in his mid-fifties and Al in his early sixties, but as Mike says, "We're not old...we're experienced."

As the most "experienced" member of the team, Al is well respected. Over the years, even as the captains have changed, Al has always been the unofficial team coach, offering advice and instruction to anyone who requests it. Everyone appreciates receiving pointers from Al because his teaching style is low key and cordial. I think of Al as the wise old man sitting on top of a mountain, dispensing sage advice to anyone who ventures to the mountain top. In reality though, Al's mountain is the Albany tennis courts.

On Dale's team last year, Mike and Al were buried on the depth chart, rarely ever playing in important matches. With the loss of many of our top doubles players, I thought Mike and Al could be a key team this year. Many people underestimate them because they are not a flashy team. They just play smart, figuring out their opponents' weaknesses and then feasting on them. It can be a winning strategy at the 4.0 level. With Ross and Chris about six feet tall and in excellent physical shape, it was a classic matchup of brains vs. brawn.

Brawn never had a chance. It took all of one game for Mike and Al to figure out that Chris was the weak link. They kept making him hit one more shot until Chris would eventually smack a shot long or into the net. Ross and Chris were figuratively and literally "schooled" on the court, losing 6-2, 6-4 while receiving doubles position pointers from Al.

Youth was served a bit of humble pie on court #2 as well. Although Billy is a more talented tennis player than Doc, there was far more rust on Billy's game. Doc, whose retirement has done wonders for his tennis game, triumphed 6-3, 6-3 over the guy I had built our entire home schedule around. Every time I looked at their court, the Kid looked frustrated, muttering to himself as he adjusted his racket strings. Intensely competitive, he hates losing, even in practice. At the end of the second set, Billy rushed off the court saying he had to leave to get to band practice. You'd think he'd want to stay away from musical instruments for the rest of the day after getting beaten like a drum on the court.

On court #3, I had several players rotating in and out, including six foot tall Matt. Once a college pitcher, Matt is a pure athlete. Wearing his customary worn out Yankees cap and old t-shirt, Matt serves like he used to pitch, mixing in spins with his power serve. Now in his late thirties, he has decided to settle down, announcing his engagement to his girlfriend of three years. In previous years, Matt had played singles for us, but I told him that my first strategic move as captain was to transform him into a doubles player. With his big serve and congenial personality, I felt his game was more suited for doubles. In his usual easy going manner, he replied, "Sure, I guess my single days are over, on and off the court."

After the practice, newcomer Chris came up to me. He told me he's played sporadically for the last ten years, but never competitively. "I'm sorry. I played horrible today. I saw you watching us and I got nervous."

"Nervous? Why were you nervous?"

"I wanted to impress you. Show you why you'd want me on the team."

"First of all, you're on the team. Sign up tonight. Second of all, just relax and enjoy playing tennis. Life is too short to get nervous about a game of tennis."

Chris nodded his head and smiled. He jogged over and said something to his buddy Ross before they exchanged a high five.

Ross came over to thank me. He explained that he and Chris had been best friends since junior high school. Close teammates on several high school sports teams and best man at each other's weddings, Ross and Chris were like brothers. Ross smiled broadly as he talked about Chris moving back in the area a couple of months ago.

As captain, I felt like I made a good move to keep my #1 doubles player happy. Still, I wondered if I would later regret my decision.

The USTA released the regular season schedules, showing ten teams in our East Bay league. Competing once a week, we were scheduled to play each team once for a total of nine matches. The adult league format is simple. In each team match, there are a total of five individual matches, three doubles and two singles. The team that wins at least three individual matches wins the overall team match.

At the end of the regular season, the four teams with the best overall match records advance to the local league playoffs. The #1 seed will host the #4 seed while the #2 seed will host the #3 seed in the first round. Then, the winners will compete for the league championships. Next, league champions move on to the District Championships to face other league champions. After Districts, survivors advance to the Sectional Championships and, finally, Nationals.

Based on previous years, you have a good idea which teams will be your toughest opponents. You'd like to ease into the season with weaker opponents, but the USTA scheduled three strong opponents to start our season. Our first opponent was a solid Alameda team, followed by last year's #1 seed San Leandro, and then co-defending league champ Union City.

Alameda and Opening Day

Chinese philosopher Lao-tzu said, "A journey of a thousand miles begins with one step." I was hoping we did not trip on our first step against Alameda, a perennial contending team that hailed from an expensive club. They have 19 newly surfaced tennis courts at their posh facility, but we had an advantage playing at home. Our three courts, yes count 'em, three, were in the middle of a park. Club players used to playing in a quiet, serene environment have to adapt to the noises of music playing, basketballs bouncing, and kids screaming. It looked like we'd have a special treat for our opponents this week: dog training. There were about twenty barking dogs just behind the tennis courts getting training lessons today.

Moments before my first match as captain, I must confess to some butterflies. I desperately wanted to start off with a win. At the beginning of the match, each captain fills out a lineup card indicating who is playing #1 singles, #2 singles, #1 doubles, #2 doubles, and #3 doubles. Theoretically, captains should put their stronger players at the higher seeded spot so each team's best singles player match up against each other, and so on. However, there is no rule requiring this.

Thus, many captains engage in "stacking", which means they intentionally play stronger teams at lower positions. Suppose you are playing the card game "War", where you play one card at a time and the highest card wins. You have a ten, eight, and two in your hand while your opponent has a king, nine, and seven in his hand. You clearly have the weaker overall hand and if you both agree to play the cards in order of strength, his king beats your ten, his nine beats your eight, and his seven easily beats your two. But… if you play the two card first, then the ten and eight, you actually win two of the three and feel like a genius.

As captain, I'm not above "stacking" in a key match, but the problem is that you never know how your opponent will line up. In singles, Billy took the decision away from me. Because of his band, he had to play right at 10:00 AM so he played #1 singles and Doc played #2 singles. I played Ross and Chris at #1 doubles, hoping they would be matched against Alameda's best team. Call it tough love, but I didn't think Ross and Chris would be one of our top doubles teams and the best way to show Ross was for them to lose.

When we exchanged lineups, I learned that I guessed correctly. They played their strongest team at #1 doubles. Smiling on the inside, I shook the Alameda captain's hand and then pointed out the court each match would play. Since we only have three courts for our home matches, we start with #1 singles and the top two doubles.

A relaxed, unassuming school administrator by day, my doubles partner Matt is a fierce competitor on the court. He is pretty much a sponge ready to absorb any information and tips related to playing doubles. I told him the most important rule to win in doubles: come to the net.

I read somewhere that if you have two teams of equal ability the team that controls the net will win 90% of the time. I don't know about you, but to me that sounds like a completely made up stat. Nonetheless, it makes the point. Coming to the net puts pressure on your opponents to hit a passing shot or a perfect lob. If they are unsuccessful, the chances of winning the next shot via a winning overhead or angle volley are much better than hitting a winner from the baseline. Our attacking style and some well timed dog barks on a few of our opponents' second serves netted us a 6-4, 6-4 win.

As soon as I got off the court, I called Stacey to give her the news.

"That's great," she said. "See, everything worked out. I told you that you worry too much."

"Well, I've won my match," I said over the phone. "But, we still have to win two more for the team to win. And we've lost the first sets in both of the other two matches currently going on."

Stacey sighed. "Would you just relax and enjoy the rest of the match, please?"

"Yes, ma'am," I said with a smile. "I'll be at your house by 7:00 tonight. Love you. Bye."

After I hung up, I watched the conclusion of Ross and Chris' match. Their debut was a rocky one. Ross is a really good 4.0 doubles player with a great serve, textbook ground strokes, and aggressive net play. Unfortunately, Chris struggled, but facing Alameda's top doubles team had a lot to do with it. The Alameda duo put pressure on our guys, attacking the net, dictating the point, and forcing Chris to come up with difficult shots. Our guys lost 6-4, 6-1.

Both our singles players were locked in epic battles against young opponents with endless energy. It was nerve-racking watching Billy's match, figuring that the overall match might be determined by it. I stood alone, leaning up against the fence for the entire third set, agonizing over every long rally. I even noticed my hand shaking before I gripped the fence tighter. On match point, I cheered loudly when Billy hit a baseline winner to complete an exciting 3-6, 6-4, 6-4 comeback win before bolting for band practice. In the later matches, Doc, wearing his trademark visor, took on another youthful foe. Cheered on by his gorgeous wife who wore skimpy clothing, shades and a hat in the hot sun, Doc played outstandingly, outlasting a very tough opponent 6-4, 2-6, 6-3.

Mike and Al completed the 4-1 win, pulling out a tough match 7-5, 7-5. After the match, both teams enjoyed the cold cut sandwiches, chips, vegetable platter, sodas, and beer. The highlight was Doc's wife's chili casserole dish. As the home team, we provide the food and drinks, and I take pride in putting out an impressive spread. I'm not fond of teams whose "food and drinks" include a bag of stale chips and directions to a nearby water fountain. Several Alameda players told an even worse story about a San Jose team that dubbed themselves the "Dream Team" this year. The captain of the "Dream Team" sent visiting teams an email at the beginning of this season saying that they would not be providing food and drinks because they were saving money for their trip to Nationals. That's a good way to motivate a visiting team.

A captain must wear many hats. Captains are coaches, chauffeurs, psychologists, event planners, cooks, hosts, and journalists. I put on the journalist hat after every match to write an email to the team detailing the results. It's a nice recognition of the players in the match and a good update to teammates who may have missed the match. It takes a special art to write these emails. You want to paint your players' effort and play in the best possible light, yet still have the write-up qualify as nonfiction.

After hitting the send button on the email, I had officially gotten through my first match as captain. Every USTA team falls somewhere on the spectrum of being a team "just out to have fun" or a competitive team that is going all out for a league championship. My mantra was, "We're just out to have fun, but since we think winning is fun, that's what we'll do."

So far, so good.

One of the best aspects of USTA leagues is that you can join it along with a friend. I started league play with Gary, a close friend and former college roommate. Back when we started ten years ago, Gary was single and we were known as the "young guns". Since then, I became best man at his wedding and later "uncle" to his two kids. We have assembled an impressive USTA record, playing in 40 matches and winning 33 of them.

Not wanting to rest on my laurels of a 1-0 team record, I decided to literally call in a favor.

"Hi Gary. It's Eric."

"How's it going?" Gary asked over high-pitched noises in the background.

"Is this a good time?"

"You mean, when there's no screaming and crying? Do you want to call back in ten years?"

"No," I said with a chuckle. "I need to ask a big favor now. I really need you to play on my 4.0 Albany team. I think the team could use your help and I really want to see this team succeed."

"It's going to be tough. With the two boys and the crazy hours at work, I'm pretty busy." Gary paused and I resisted the temptation to interrupt the silence. "But, if it's important to you, I'll play in as many matches as I can."

"Thanks Gary. Are you available this Saturday at 10:00 AM? We play San Leandro and they're really good."

Gary laughed. "You don't waste any time, do ya? Alright. I'll make it work."

San Leandro and Breaking Up a Doubles Team

On Tuesday before I announced our lineup against our arch rival San Leandro, I received a call from Ross. Over the years, I have become friends with Ross so it was not unusual to talk to him during the week. But, this call was all business.

"Are you planning on playing me against San Leandro?" he asked.

"Of course. Their strength is in doubles and you're our best doubles player. We need to win this match."

"Okay, I'd like to play with Chris again."

"I said we needed to win this match."

Ross let out an audible sigh, finding little humor in my remark. "Look, we practiced this evening. He played great. He was just nervous in his first USTA match."

"What makes you think he wouldn't be nervous in his second USTA match? I was thinking we'd rest him and play him against a weaker opponent." When a captain says he is going to "rest" a player during the regular season, that's a nice way of saying he's benched. We only play once a week. How much rest does someone need?

"You're the captain, but I'm asking for one more chance. We'll win this week. I guarantee it."

I paused to think as I ran my fingers through my hair. Ross' loyalty to Chris was both admirable and annoying. "Okay," I said reluctantly before we hung up.

The next night, after sending out the lineup, I got a call from my co-captain Barry. "Why are we playing Chris again? We have other players that have yet to play. Besides, Chris isn't ready, especially at #1 doubles. It's like you're setting him up to fail."

"It's what Ross wants," I said. "And if they get crushed at #1 doubles, Ross will be convinced that he should play with someone better. The break-up of the Ross-Chris tandem will help the team in the long run."

"I don't see how crushing Chris' confidence could be a good thing for him or the team. Here's my advice. Worry less about wins and losses and more about team camaraderie and happiness."

"Okay Barry," I said, freely rolling my eyes since I was on the phone. "I'll see you at the match this Saturday."

We played our next match against San Leandro on our home courts, scheduled on Saturday at 10:00 AM so Billy could play. It was the second week in a row that we would host a club team unaccustomed to playing on public courts. No dog training this week at the Albany park, but distractions included a noisy pickup basketball game. I was using the same lineup as the first match with one change, inserting Gary for Matt.

My girlfriend Stacey arrived right at match time to cheer me on. "How do you feel?" Stacey asked.

"Nervous. I'm hoping that I have the right matchups with the lineup."

"You need to relax. This is recreational tennis. It's supposed to be about having fun, not creating stress. Where's the other captain?"

I pointed out Jeff, the San Leandro captain, who casually talked with a teammate. Every time that I have seen Jeff he is dressed the same way, wearing a baseball cap and sunglasses.

"He doesn't look like he's stressing out," Stacey said. "Be like him."

I nodded, realizing I could learn something from a cool, calculating captain like Jeff. He embodies the Michael Caine quote. "Be like a duck. Calm on the surface, but always paddling like the dickens underneath."

I gave Stacey a quick kiss and walked over to Jeff. "Ready to exchange lineups?"

"Yep," Jeff said as we handed each other our lineup card. I think Jeff is the best captain in our league. He is intensely competitive and seems laser-focused on his goal to win the league. I heard he has his club pro attend his practices and give pointers to his players. San Leandro's strongest doubles team is the Chang twins, and Gary and I were matched up against them at #2 doubles. Darn it. Jeff noticed I put a weaker team at #1 doubles last week and he figured I would do it again.

The Chang twins possess the perfect game to frustrate aggressive players like Gary and me. They had offensive topspin lobs that easily cleared our heads, but then dove down inside the baseline, and finally took off, making it nearly impossible to chase down. Gary and I were completely thrown off our game plan and we were beaten 6-2, 6-4. Stacey greeted me at the gate with a hug and a kiss, but my mind was preoccupied with my two botched overheads in the last game.

"It's okay. They were a tough team," Stacey said, sensing I needed cheering up. "Let's go and get lunch at the Chinese restaurant."

"I can't go. I have to stay for the entire match."

She crossed her arms. I loved Stacey for her looks, but not the one she was giving me now. "Why?" she asked. "Do you have to stay and organize practices? Do you have to determine lineups?" I know Stacey well. She was using sarcasm to mask her frustration. "Just remember, you've made other commitments too," she added before turning to leave.

I got the message loud and clear. She was not happy about how much of my time had been usurped by becoming captain. I knew I would have to do damage control tonight. After she left, we went on to split the other two early matches. Billy was in control of his match throughout, winning 6-3, 6-3. Ross and Chris lost 6-4, 7-6 with Chris double faulting three times in the tiebreaker, the last of the three on match point. Ross walked off the court first and as he passed me, he said softly, "You were right. He's not match ready."

As Ross walked away, I couldn't help but smile. I had achieved my goal. He wouldn't be pressing me any more to play with Chris in big matches. My smile quickly disappeared when I noticed Chris still sitting on the bench, head down, alone. As a captain and strategist, I'm reminded that I am not playing with a deck of cards. I'm playing with real people who have real emotions. I thought about what Barry said about keeping the team happy.

I walked over to Chris and sat down next to him. "Tough match."

"I'm a choke artist. I just can't play well during matches," Chris said, looking at the ground.

"Hey, it's just a setback. Think of it as a learning opportunity. You just have to pick yourself up, dust yourself off, and come back stronger next time. I'll work with you in match situations over the next couple of practices and I bet Al would be happy to give you some technical advice on your strokes. So, don't worry about it, okay?" Chris looked up at me and nodded. "Hey," I said, slapping Chris on the back. "We can still win this match if Doc comes through in singles and Mike and Al win their doubles match. Come on, let's root them on."

San Leandro and Breaking Up a Doubles Team

Mike and Al, bless their experienced hearts, played a smart, consistent game in winning a thriller 6-4, 7-6 to tie the overall match score at two. That left Doc, who split his first two sets, to play a final set that would determine the entire match. I felt confident Doc would pull it out, because he was playing a far weaker opponent than the player he beat last week. With all the players, and friends and family of players watching this match, an estimated sixty people were cheering on almost every point.

I could barely watch the final set. I got up and paced for a while. Then, I would sit down and watch with my hands clasped. I closed my eyes and said a prayer, "God, I know you're busy with the requests to end world hunger and devastating wars. But since this is such a simple request, I thought you could push it to the top of your list. Just let us win this tiebreaker so we can start the season 2-0." Unfortunately, Doc played a very poor set, uncharacteristically hitting a ton of unforced errors. He never got into rhythm and lost 6-1.

We broke out the sandwiches, chips, assorted fruit, and drinks. Our guys did our best to console a distraught Doc. Mike did it in the best way he knew how, needling him. "Doc, you brought chips and store-bought salsa. Where's the great casserole dish your wife made last week?"

"Sorry, she didn't have time this week," Doc said with a shrug.

Soda in hand, I walked over to congratulate a much more relaxed Jeff who said, "It was a good win for us considering we had three of our best guys in San Jose playing a tennis tournament." I'm not sure why Jeff brought this up except to make clear that his team was far superior since he beat us without his best players. It revealed Jeff's ego and the fact that our playoff upset last year still annoyed him. "So who do you guys play next?" Jeff asked.

"Union City."

"Oh, man. Your team is going to take a beating," Jeff said, undermining our team's tennis ability. "I watched their first match of the season. Union City crushed Berkeley 5-0." Jeff kept talking, but I was struck by the fact he took time out of his weekend to scout a regular season match in the first week of the season. He was either really committed or really needed to be committed, at a local institution. How could I possibly compete with captains like this? I turned my attention back to Jeff, who was still talking. "Union City has two doubles teams that are outstanding. Best I've ever seen at 4.0. At singles, they've got a kid named Ace and another guy named Brian."

"Wait a minute. They have a kid named Ace?"

"Yeah, he's a self rated 4.0 player, but he could play as a 5.0 he's so good. Their other singles player, Brian, is a ringer too. All around great game, his only weakness I can see is that he hasn't built up his singles stamina, so if a really good player can extend him to three sets, maybe he'll get tired. Problem is not many legitimate 4.0 players will be able to take a set from that guy."

"What's Ace's weakness?"

With little expression on his face, Jeff slowly shook his head. "He doesn't have one."

As I drove home, I felt a little depressed. It's not that I lost my first match as captain. It's that the team lost 3 to 2 and I lost my individual match. I felt I let the team down as a player and a captain. I began to contemplate the "what ifs", the best form of personal torture. What if I played better in my match? What if I would have done the line up in a different order? And what if I played Ross with someone else?

By the next evening, I felt much better about the loss to San Leandro. The anticipation of Stacey coming over had a way of lifting my spirits. Normally, we cook dinner together, but Stacey arrived looking stressed and exhausted.

"I've been up since 7:00 AM doing research on a case," Stacey announced, collapsing on the couch.

I sat down beside her, massaging her neck. "Just relax. We don't have to cook. We can order from the Chinese restaurant that you wanted to eat at yesterday."

"That sounds good," Stacey said with a smile.

I kissed her neck and shoulders before I asked, "What's going on at work?"

"I'm on a new client, who is being sued. I've been swamped. I just found out that I have to be in Los Angeles for a week, starting Wednesday."

"So, you won't be around next weekend?" I asked, temporarily stopping the massage.

"Unfortunately, no," Stacey said.

"I'll miss you," I said before asking her to lie down on the sofa as I massaged her feet. She closed her eyes and it appeared that she was beginning to relax. I enjoyed taking care of her.

Stacey said, "I don't know why I work so hard: the long hours and the traveling, just to make partner."

"I thought it was your dream to make partner."

"No, this, you massaging my feet, is my dream." I chuckled before she added, "As partner, I'll make more money, but ultimately I'll just have to work even more hours. I want something more from life, you know. Eventually, I want to settle down and raise a family. I want the big front lawn with the picket fence, 2.2 kids, and a dog. But right now, I'd settle for more time with you."

"Well, how does this sound? The Friday after you come back from L.A., we go away overnight at a resort in Carmel, just the two of us."

She smiled broadly and said, "That sounds perfect."

Union City and Team Turmoil

Next to a roster filled with ringers, the most valuable asset to a successful captain is his co-captain. Someone who can run a practice or a league match if the captain can't make it. Equally important, someone with whom you can discuss major roster decisions and lineup calls. My co-captain, Barry, has been a captain for several teams that have made it to the prestigious District Championships. As a 3.5 a couple of years ago, Barry played in the National Championships.

You know the angel and devil that sits on each of your shoulders? Barry is the angel. Average height with a skinny frame, Barry always has a trimmed beard and mustache with a baseball cap over his balding head. He displays a pleasant disposition, highlighted by his friendly smile and soft spoken laugh. He has a sharp tennis mind, but an even better heart. He always wants to make sure everyone on the team feels like they have been treated fairly. Although he would like the team to succeed, he still says nutty things like, "It's just a game" and, "It's all about having fun."

My tennis cabinet also includes Lloyd, who has been a captain on many 4.0 teams that have won at Districts as well. The clean shaven Lloyd plays the role of the devil on my shoulder. That sounds harsh since he is one of the nicest guys you would ever want to meet. However, like me, he is competitive and when he sees an opportunity to win a league championship, he believes you should go for it. He once said, "Don't worry about pleasing everyone. Win a league championship and everyone will be pleased." Like a silent assassin, Lloyd is soft-spoken and respectful while trying everything to be successful.

If Barry and Lloyd were ever cast on the television show *Survivor*, Lloyd would do whatever it took to win, including scheming, and making and breaking alliances. "If it's within the rules, then it's fair," Lloyd would say. On the other hand, Barry would preach to the camera the importance of having integrity and showing loyalty to friends, just before he was voted off the island first... by Lloyd.

At practice, Billy was sporting a new haircut. Mike whistled and asked, "What's with the new look, Kid?"

"I have an interview this Friday at Craig's law firm. I figured I'd spiff myself up a bit. I even dusted the cobwebs off my suit."

"You just might pass for a lawyer yet," Craig said.

"For today though, I'm just a tennis player," a smiling Billy said as he put on his baseball cap and led Craig to one of the upper courts. It was great to see the relationship between Craig and Billy. Although it was Craig who had helped Billy professionally, I could overhear Billy politely giving Craig pointers on his service motion. The two clearly had a mutual respect for each other.

On the lower court, I had Chris play a bunch of 10 point tiebreaker doubles matches. Sometimes I watched. Sometimes I played with him and sometimes I played against him. We talked about "living in the moment", blocking everything else out, and concentrating on his task at hand. After I worked on the mental side, Al took him to a separate court to work on his volley technique.

After practice, Barry, Lloyd, and I met for dinner to discuss our lineup against Union City, who had won their first two matches 5-0. The match was at Union City's courts at noon on Sunday, which meant Billy couldn't make it because he had what he called a "gig". Have I mentioned that I hate bands and now all music?

To make matters worse, my partner Gary was unavailable for the match because of his son's 1st birthday party. My argument that his son won't remember any of it and my suggestion that we could photoshop him into the pictures didn't fly with him or his wife.

"We have to get some new guys in the lineup," Barry said.

"I want to play our very best against Union City," I said. "Jeff from San Leandro thinks we'll get crushed. I want to send a message to the entire league by beating these guys."

Barry looked disappointed. "We've got guys that haven't even played yet, like Ron. He's a solid doubles player."

I replied, "Ron isn't as strong as anyone we have in the lineup. We can get him and others some playing time over the next two weeks when we play weaker opponents."

Lloyd nodded his approval while Barry begrudgingly gave in.

Lloyd looked at me. "So, do you think we have the guys that can beat Union City?"

"Of course we don't," Barry said, answering for me. "But who cares? This season isn't about beating Union City."

"That's what the season could be about," I said with raised eyebrows.

"Exactly," Lloyd said. "If we add a new player, it could put us over the top. I'm thinking of a guy named Steve. He has played for Albany before."

"You two are living in fantasy land," Barry said, rising from the table. "This Steve could be Pete Sampras. We still wouldn't have the team to compete with Union City."

Barry left to go the restroom and I said to Lloyd, "How come I've never heard of Steve?"

"He's only played in mixed leagues over the last three years."

The mixed league is a doubles only league where each doubles team has one woman and one man. There are many reasons people prefer mixed. Some people do it to get out and hit with their wives. Others do it to get out and meet their future wife. Sounds like a dangerous proposition to me. Remember, in tennis, love means nothing. In fact, the only people I know who really love mixed tennis are divorce attorneys.

"So why does he only play mixed?"

"He didn't always," Lloyd said. "He used to play tournaments and adult leagues. He's a real nice guy off the court, but on the court, he's super intense. One time he really lost it. He was playing poorly and began tossing his racket and shouting at himself. He got married and now he only plays in mixed leagues. He likes it because it is mellower and doesn't get him all worked up."

"You think we can get him on our team?"

"It's worth a try. He'd be our best doubles player. He's that good."

"Okay, call Steve and invite him on the team. Hopefully he can play against Union City."

The most anticipated match of the regular season arrived on Sunday. It was a beautiful day for tennis with sunny skies and temperatures in the high seventies. Union City treated every home USTA match as an event. They had a large crowd of teammates, family, and friends in attendance. I'd estimate that their crowd outnumbered ours 50 to 3. Besides Barry and me, our only other Albany faithful was Craig's 11 year-old son, who bolted for the nearby playground as soon as the matches started. Stacey was out of town for the weekend on business travel.

Even Doc's wife, a vocal mainstay in our fan base, missed this match.

I wanted to watch all of the matches so I did not put myself in the lineup. During warm-ups, I studied the Union City players. They were co-league champions last year and won at the District Championships. With that success, the USTA moved a lot of their players up to 4.5 making them ineligible for 4.0 leagues. As I watched this new crop of Union City players, all I could think of was a star fish. You know, the sea creature. You can cut off a piece of a star fish, but it magically just grows the piece back as strong as before. These guys were impressive. They not only hit the ball with the authority and accuracy of a champion, they carried themselves as champions with a sense of quiet confidence.

As home to one of the largest public parks in the Bay Area, Union City is a tennis factory. Their captain, a retired tennis pro, runs several Union City league teams without actually playing. In the offseason, he runs tennis camps and clinics, which bring him fresh crops of tennis players who he can sign up for league play.

We exchanged lineups and I gathered the team together for a quick meeting. Craig, our third best singles player, was making his season debut with Billy unavailable. Craig, a quick, smart player, still packs a wallop in his small frame. I told him that he was facing some guy named Ace that I did not know much about. I left out the part that he has a 5.0 game with no weaknesses. I got the match-up I wanted in the other singles match as Doc faced a guy in his late 20s named Brian. I was hoping Doc would pull out his match and we would win two of the three doubles with the following teams playing: Ross and Matt, Lloyd and Steve, and Mike and Al. I was both excited and nervous about the big match. I had to remind myself to calm down.

Steve came up to me after our team briefing. Built like a linebacker and wearing a black tank top that accentuated his muscular frame, Steve had an imposing presence. "Thanks for the opportunity to play with you guys."

"Glad to have you with us," I said, shaking his hand.

As all five matches took the courts, I knew things were now out of my control. To calm my nerves, I headed to the grill. Union City easily had the best spread of food in the league. They would barbeque hamburgers, hot dogs, and chicken to go along with coolers filled with every drink you can think of. I got a freshly cooked hamburger, some chips, and bottled water. By the time I finished my hamburger, Ace spun his racket and Craig won the right to serve first. It was about the only thing he won all day. I have never seen a player in a 4.0 league like Ace. He moved Craig all over the court and demolished him 6-0 in the first set. As another serve whistled by a lunging Craig, I chuckled at this kid's name. It's like his family knew he was going to be a tennis star when he came out of the womb.

Things weren't any better on the other courts. We dropped the first set in all five of the matches with only Lloyd and Steve's 6-3 score being respectable. Sitting next to co-captain Barry, I just shook my head in disbelief as I watched Ace continue to take Craig apart. It was getting even worse... and I thought it couldn't... but Craig was getting tired running down Ace's missiles.

The Union City captain was an older gentleman named Pablo. As I watched the match, a smiling Pablo kept coming by offering more food and drink. "Would you like another hamburger, my friend? Want something else to drink, my friend?" Even though Pablo was clearly a nice guy and a great host, he was no friend of mine. Friends don't humiliate other friends' tennis team.

After about ten minutes, the pit of my stomach hurt as I saw all our doubles suffer early breaks in the second set. I turned to

Barry. "My stomach's bothering me. I don't know if it's these matches or indigestion."

"I hope it's indigestion."

"Why?"

"Because then it'll get better in awhile."

I was too depressed to laugh. Barry's words were prophetic. We quickly proceeded to drop the two singles matches. Despite the wide variety of food Union City brought, only Craig was treated to two bagels (6-0, 6-0). Still, if a few bounces would've gone Craig's way, you never know, he could have won... a game. Doc, who played a particularly poor match, tossed his lucky visor in frustration after his 6-1, 6-1 loss.

Union City's doubles were outstanding. Their #1 and #2 doubles were a clear level above any of our teams. They each lost only two games in total during their demolition of Ross and Matt at #1 doubles and Mike and Al at #2 doubles. The lone bright spot of the day was seeing Steve's potential. Absent from competitive play for a while, he started off rusty. But, once he got in the flow of the match, he displayed some real power tennis, smacking aces and smoking forehand winners. I didn't witness any racket throwing. There were a few times, especially early, that Steve appeared frustrated with himself, but Lloyd would walk over and talk to him and then he seemed fine. Steve is a gamer who gives his all on the court, even diving after a ball. I think he wears any scrape as a badge of honor. After losing the first set, Lloyd and Steve won our only set of the day 7-5 before falling in the third 6-4.

So, we got swept 5-0. Union City didn't just beat us. They destroyed us, making it impossible to envision a scenario where we could ever win 3 of 5 individual matches against them. Our overall record fell to 1-2. It was particularly frustrating for me. Starting off the season 1-2 is never good, but usually you can say that you are just having fun. You're losing not because you stink as a captain. It's because you're being such a nice guy who lets everyone play. Everyone loves a winner. People also love a 1-2 nice guy who lets everyone play. But, no one likes a 1-2 jerk that plays the same guys in almost every match. And that's what I'd been doing.

After the match concluded, I got a call from my dad on my cell phone. "How did you do today?"

"The team lost," I said as I made my way to my car.

"How did you do?"

"I didn't play."

"Why not? If you're going to go through all the hassles of being captain, you might as well play."

"I just wanted to watch this week, dad."

"Ok, did you see the doctor like you promised?"

"I have an appointment next week," I said, mentally noting that now I had to schedule an appointment for next week. When I reached my car, I told my dad that I would talk to him more tonight.

On my ride home, I realized that I would have to relive the beating we just took when I did the email write-up. The task to paint a positive light on our guys play today might be as difficult a task as trying to defeat the ringer-filled Union City team. I mean, how do you make a 6-0, 6-0 defeat sound good?

That night, I reviewed the standings. With only the top four teams advancing to the playoffs, I realized that we had a lot of work to do, mired in seventh place. I took solace in the fact that we had finished playing three of the top four teams, based on the current standings.

We were three matches into a nine-match season. Here is how the East Bay league standings stood with the win-loss record and individual match wins in brackets.

1. Union City   3-0   [15]
2. San Leandro 3-0   [13]
3. Hayward   3-0   [11]
4. Alameda   2-1   [10]

5. Piedmont	2-1	[7]
6. Oakland	1-2	[7]
7. Albany	1-2	[6]
8. Berkeley	0-3	[3]
9. Richmond	0-3	[3]
10. Hercules	0-3	[0]

In the event of a tie in win-loss record, the team with the greater individual match wins gets the higher spot in the standings.

Later that night, I checked my email and received the following from Ron: "I have played with Albany for 3 years and consider myself a solid 4.0 player. Even though I have been available, you have refused to play me in any of the first three matches. I am left to conclude that my tennis services are not appreciated on this team. Given that, I prefer not to be a part of this team any more. Please take me off the email distribution list. Thank you."

My heart dropped as I stared at the computer screen. I did not see this coming and I began to feel very guilty. On impulse, I picked up the phone to call him. I wanted to tell him that I was sorry. I wanted to tell him that I'd put him in the next match. But, I never had the chance. As soon as Ron realized it was me, he said, "I don't want to talk about it. I've made up my mind. Please don't call back again."

Stunned, I held the phone in my hand for a few moments after he hung up. This was exactly the reason that I did not want to be the captain. At least one friend was now an enemy all because of playing time. I thought about the Ron incident all night. Any way you look at it, I screwed up. The team is not winning and players aren't happy. Maybe I wasn't cut out to be captain, at least not now.

After thinking about it for most of the next day, I decided that I should step down as captain. I don't consider myself a quitter, but this seemed best for the team and me. I knew it would make Stacey happy if I had more free time. I called Barry to tell him what happened with Ron and ask that he take over for me as captain.

"You want to quit as captain? Why?"

"I've been a failure. Players are quitting. The team is losing. We were league champions last year under Dale. This year, we are in 7th place."

"The schedule gets easier. We'll climb the standings."

"Dale would have the team in first place now."

There was a momentary silence on the phone. "Wait a minute. You don't know?"

"Know what?"

"Why Dale didn't want to captain this year."

"Yeah, I do. It was because he got moved down to 3.5."

"Yeah, that's part of it. But, if this were truly a league championship team, Dale still would have captained it. Knowing how many people were not coming back from last year, Dale thought this team would be lucky to win half its matches. This is just a 'for fun' team."

How could I be the only one blind to the fact that this team was only for fun? Since we were co-league champs last year and given Albany's history of success, I assumed everyone expected us to at least contend for the league title. I remained speechless as Barry continued.

"You've done such a good job recruiting, first Gary and then Steve. Billy is playing better than anyone expected. The guys really respect you as a captain. Please, don't quit."

I paused a moment to process everything Barry was saying. "Alright, alright. I'll stay on."

Berkeley and Staying Healthy

Sometimes, mental health is more important than physical health. Stacey and I left work early on Friday to travel south for some much needed rest and relaxation at a posh resort in Carmel, a city on the California coastline. I planned the entire trip. After a spa treatment, candlelit dinner, and a romantic night together, I think Stacey had forgotten all about her stressful work week. It was also cathartic for me to occupy my mind with things other than Albany's 1-2 start and Ron's angry exodus.

On Saturday morning, we slept in and ordered room service for breakfast. After breakfast, we sat out on our balcony admiring a splendid coastline view. Sipping some coffee, she turned to me and said, "I'm really starting to re-evaluate my career goals, like whether it really makes sense for me to try to make partner. When we have kids sometime in the next five years, I'm going to want to stay home with them until they go to preschool."

I looked at Stacey not knowing how to respond. We have had the "marriage" talk and the "kid" talk and we agreed that's where we're headed. We just haven't agreed on the exact timing. Admittedly, I had been the one dragging my feet. I'm still not sure I could ever picture myself as a father, but I could tell by how often she brings up the "children" word, she was ready. I decided to steer the conversation back toward her career. I put my arm around her and said, "I'll support you in whatever you decide for your career, but my vote is that you do whatever makes you happy."

Stacey looked back at the coastline. "I guess that's what I have to figure out." We spent a great day at the beach and touring the city on Saturday before I dropped Stacey off at her house late Saturday night.

Renewed and refreshed from my Carmel trip, I woke up the next morning expecting our next match to be stress-free. After all, we were playing against an 0-3 Berkeley team that was also cursed with a difficult opening schedule. I took this opportunity to play a lot of doubles players who had yet to play. To clear playing time this week, I benched Billy, Matt, Ross, Gary, and myself. Because Berkeley had weak singles players, I felt Doc and Craig would easily win and I felt confident that we would win at least one doubles match.

Playing on the road at Berkeley on Sunday, we were able to play all five at once. Doc, who didn't have his pretty wife present to cheer him on, nonetheless prevailed in an error-filled 7-5, 6-4 victory. Despite the win, it was clear Doc had not played well. We split #1 and #2 doubles to take an overall 2-1 match lead. We needed just one more win. Relegated to a fan this week, I watched the matches from the shade to escape from the blistering 100 degree temperatures. Although we had dropped the first set in a tiebreaker at #3 doubles, Craig was cruising at #2 singles. So, no worries. Craig was up 6-2, 5-1 when disaster struck. On the first point of the seventh game, I heard him cry out in agony as he went to the ground. Doc and I raced over toward him.

"It's my thigh," Craig said, grimacing in pain. We quickly realized that he was suffering from severe leg cramps.

Doc asked someone to retrieve a banana from the food table. He then proceeded to drop electrolyte pills that fizzed into his large water bottle. "Here, drink this. All of it," Doc ordered, handing him the bottle. When someone handed Doc a banana, he added, "Eat this."

As Craig's 40 year old body relaxed, his leg no longer spasmed, and the pain subsided. As several players towered over their fallen teammate, Doc began lecturing Craig on the importance of being hydrated, especially on hot days.

I helped Craig to his feet, hoping he could somehow still play, but he cramped up again after taking a few steps. Doc announced, "That's it. You're done for the day."

If this were a professional match, we would have shot Craig up with something so he could make it through those final games. But, we aren't pros and have a smaller medical budget.

I knew Craig, a fierce player and former US Marine, had a higher than normal pain tolerance. I pulled him aside for a moment. "You're up 5-1 in the set, right?" Craig nodded. "We really need one more win. Do you think you can hang in there for the team and see if you can win one of these next four games?"

"I don't know," Craig said as he massaged his leg.

"Hey, it's up to you. But, I'd like you to try to finish it."

Craig took a deep breath and exhaled slowly. "I'll give it a try."

When Craig picked up his racket, Doc immediately protested, "What are you doing? You shouldn't play. You can do more damage to your leg muscles."

"I want to try," Craig responded.

When Doc looked at me for support, I just said, "It's his call."

Doc looked shocked and disappointed.

Eventually everyone left the court and Craig resumed his match up 5-1 in the second set, but down 15-love. After Craig's opponent missed his first serve, he served a soft second serve. Standing near the service line, Craig attacked it, smacking a winner down the line. The Albany crowd roared. However,

Doc was not applauding. Instead, he shook his head and shot me an angry glare. I refocused my attention on the match.

It was clear that Craig's tactic was to end the rally with a winner as quickly as possible. When his opponent double faulted at thirty all, Craig had remarkably earned a match point. On match point, Craig went for another winner, smacking his opponent's first serve just wide. A collective groan came over the deflated Albany crowd. Mobility cost Craig on the next two points and his opponent held serve. It was difficult for Craig to serve because he put much of his weight on his injured leg. When Craig was broken, the score was 5-3 and he went all out to win the next game. It was thirty all when his leg gave out again and he went down in pain.

Doc raced out to the court again to tend to Craig. Doc looked at me. "Enough is enough. He's risking serious damage to his leg muscle."

I bent down to a grimacing Craig and said, "Great effort, but we're going to call it." Craig nodded in agreement and then received an ovation from both teams as he was helped to the sidelines by two teammates.

The individual match score was tied at two and we were down a set in the final match. I was annoyed that a freak injury cost us an individual match we were sure to win. I was angry that we might now lose the overall match to a far inferior team, and I was livid that I could have prevented it by playing a stronger lineup. Now I know why they call it an "upset" when the better team loses.

I began to freak out that we could drop to 1-3 on the season and wondered if people would think, "We wouldn't be 1-3 if Dale were still captain." After I got done feeling sorry for myself, I refocused on #3 doubles where co-captain Barry and Al were battling back in the second set. Barry is a crafty lefty that keeps his ground strokes low. It is a surprisingly effective strategy. Buoyed by a vocal Albany crowd of twenty that consisted of teammates, family, and friends, Barry and Al took the second set to set up a winner-take-all final third set.

To add to the drama, the match was taking place on Berkeley's stadium court. A Berkeley player informed me that pro tennis stars, the Bryan brothers, had played an exhibition match on those same courts a week earlier. Barry and Al fought off two stubborn opponents, intense heat, and pressure in the spotlight to prevail 6-4 in the final set.

The team celebrated the win, while I simply felt relieved. We had survived, gotten back to .500, and reduced the possibility of a team mutiny. I continued to struggle with the perception of me as the captain and leader. I know the guys liked me, but did they respect me? I knew the best way to earn their respect as an accomplished leader is to convincingly win tennis matches. As captain, I wanted everyone to consider my name to be synonymous with success.

On the way home, I began to think about Craig. Something strange happens to you when you turn forty. Your brain and your body rarely agree on anything. Your brain still thinks you can do everything you used to do when you were twenty-five. Yet, your body constantly reminds you that you can't.

I'm 36 and if my body were a car, the manufacturer's warranty would have lasted 35 years. My eyesight has inexplicably been on the decline for the last two years. My stomach has aged way ahead of the rest of my body. It has taken on the character of a fussy old man, letting me know it no longer likes many of the foods it scarfed down happily when I was twenty. I no longer remember what it is like to feel 100% healthy for tennis matches. Either my shoulder, elbow, ankle, foot, you name it, it's a little sore. It takes longer for injuries to heal too, and you have to do things I would never do when I was younger, like seriously stretch before the match. I now regularly have ice bags on some part of my body after the match.

Ever since the Union City match, my stomach had been bothering me. Thus, it was good timing that on Monday, a day after the Berkeley match, I had my doctor's appointment. I received a text from Craig while I was in the waiting room.

"Saw the doctor," Craig wrote. "A lot of damage to the dehydrated muscles in my leg. Doctor says they'll heal on their own, but I'm out three weeks."

My heart dropped. I felt guilty that I even suggested that he keep playing. It hurt him and now it has hurt the team. With Doc struggling and Billy's limited availability, we were really hurting at singles. I pounded the arm of the waiting room chair in frustration.

"Eric Lee," a nurse announced.

I slowly rose and followed her into a small room. She took my weight, temperature, and blood pressure. I felt like a car in a pit stop at the Indy 500. She flashed a concerned look and said, "I'm going to take your blood pressure again." She re-strapped my arm and told me to relax. I felt the air pressure build against my arm and then drop back down. "It's pretty high," she said before noting it on my chart.

"How high?"

"180 over 103. The doctor will discuss it with you," the nurse said before exiting the room.

I waited for another five minutes before the doctor arrived. She immediately took my blood pressure. After she took the reading, she said, "It's somewhat elevated. Anything change in your life?"

I tilted my head, trying to think of anything to say other than becoming a USTA captain. Drawing a blank, I finally said, "I became captain of my tennis team."

"Uh huh," the doctor said, noting something in my chart. She proceeded with the physical exam, asking many questions. At the end of the exam, she said, "I'm going to prescribe some medication for your high blood pressure."

My heart sank. I really wanted to be able to control my blood pressure without medication. I felt like a failure.

The doctor continued to lecture me, "In addition to taking it regularly, you're going to need to watch your stress level." She said that stress could be contributing to my stomach problems as well as my high blood pressure. She suggested an over-the-counter medication for my stomach. She also gave me instructions to make an appointment with a nutritionist and attend a class on stress-reduction. Just before leaving, she said, "Tennis is a great way to get exercise. But, you need to learn to relax during your matches, or perhaps let someone else captain." So, now my doctor joined my dad and girlfriend in thinking I should call it quits.

Hercules and Acquiring a Ringer

"One of the keys to fighting high blood pressure is to reduce your sodium intake," Stacey said as she joined me on the sofa. "We should cook together more often rather than going out to eat. Most restaurants load their food with salt."

"Fine by me," I said, putting my arm around her.

Stacey rested her hand on my collarbone before unbuttoning my shirt to massage my chest. "I just want you to be healthy and I'll do whatever I can to help make that happen."

I kissed her on the forehead and said, "You're too good to me." I don't think Stacey realized it, but she had already helped immensely by being such a supportive girlfriend. Stress, which contributes to high blood pressure, increases when I worry about some outcome in my busy life. In a sea of stress, Stacey represented an island of tranquility. She provided a safe and dependable refuge to the drama and uncertainties of life and I loved her for it.

On Tuesday afternoon, she joined me for my appointment with a nutritionist. During the appointment, I had to write down my typical breakfast, lunch, and dinner. Not surprisingly, the nutritionist wanted me to make some changes. I had to say goodbye to sodas and fried foods, wheat toast replaced blueberry muffins, low fat milk switched to nonfat, and a large amount of fresh fruits and vegetables had to be in stock at my house for snacking. After the appointment, Stacey and I went grocery shopping. I had fun playfully sneaking certain less healthy items in our cart.

On Wednesday evening, instead of going to the team's weekly practice, I attended a stress reduction class at the hospital clinic. I spent most of my time worrying about what was going on at the team practice. When I was paying attention to the instructor, I heard her discussing the importance of clearing your mind. She discussed meditation and several relaxation techniques.

On Thursday, I made the phone call to inform my dad of my high blood pressure and stomach aches. I intentionally waited until I had already taken action steps related to diet and stress relief. "I'm glad you're taking steps to lead a healthier life," my dad said just before we hung up.

On Saturday, we had a match that looked to be as close to a bye as possible. We were playing a team from the city of Hercules, which ironically was very weak. In each league, you have your "haves" and your "have-nots". Hercules was definitely a "have not", as in they have not much tennis talent. The entire roster is made of 3.5s, which means they are "playing up" at the 4.0 level. I always thought that this was an interesting phrasing since while they were "playing up", they routinely got beaten down by the rest of the league. Not only did they have an overall 0-4 record, but they are 0-20 in individual matches.

Hercules, a team that could only have delusions of mediocrity, was the perfect opponent for me to practice my newfound stress-free attitude during matches. My stomach felt well enough for me to play doubles with Chris, whom I had sat out for the last two games. After taking a hand in destroying his confidence by matching him against two very tough teams, I was hoping to build it back up today.

Just before my match started, Chris and I exchanged scouting reports on our opponents. It went something like this. Forehands are erratic and weak, and the backhands are worse. I slapped him on the back and said, "You start serving. Relax and just have fun."

Chris proceeded to pound his first serve long and the second one wide. I walked over to him and said, "A double fault, eh? Was that fun?"

Chris laughed and that seemed to relax him. I learned that he's a solid player, but was simply getting psyched out in the pressure of the league match. He would mentally check out during the match, once letting his mind wander to the fact no one was eating the sandwiches that he bought. "Those were expensive," Chris said in his defense. After that, I made it a priority to say something to him between every point to help him focus, even if it was as simple as "nice shot" or "good try", or something tactical like, "Let's lob the shorter guy", or "Let's aim for the singles line to give us margin for error."

A key to being a stronger mental player is to focus in the moment and on the task. Sometimes, Chris would make an unforced error and he would still be thinking about it for several points, completely losing focus. I told him, "You can't worry about the past, and you can't think ahead to the future. You have to focus on the moment, the current point, the current shot."

How many times have you seen league players double fault in pressure situations? It's usually all mental. The player will tell himself, "don't double fault, don't double fault," and guess what they do. Instead, they should take a deep breath before they serve and focus on the court where they are going to hit the ball.

All in all, Chris played fine. He had three guys on the court helping him: me and our two Hercules opponents. The Hercules duo helped with a slew of unforced errors and we won easily.

Mike was the first to greet us off the court, asking, "What was your score?"

"We won 6-1, 6-1," Chris said, proudly.

"Hey, what happened in those two games?" Mike quipped before giving Chris a high five.

The rest of the team had it just as easy as Chris and me. We won the overall match 5-0 without dropping a set. Instead of isolating myself away from my teammates, I sat next to Mike and Chris to watch the final matches. We laughed and joked throughout the final two matches. The pizza delivery arrived in the last set of the later matches. The guys attacked the stacks of pizza like hungry wolves. I limited myself to one slice and feasted on the vegetable tray. Ah, if only I could enjoy every match as much as this one.

We had completed the fifth match in our nine match season. We're in fifth place, which was just out of the last playoff spot. The East Bay league standings now were:

1. Union City   5-0   [25]
2. San Leandro 5-0   [22]
3. Hayward   4-1   [17]
4. Alameda   3-2   [17]
5. Albany   3-2   [14]
6. Piedmont   2-3   [9]
7. Berkeley   1-4   [10]
8. Oakland   1-4   [7]
9. Richmond   0-5   [4]
10. Hercules   0-5   [0]

The good news was that we already had our match against probably the two most dominant teams in the league, Union City and San Leandro. Next week, we would draw winless Richmond before playing a tough Hayward team the following week.

That night, I had a phone conversation with Lloyd. He brought up trying to acquire a guy named Nate who would likely become the best player on our team. "Nate could play doubles as well as singles, a spot in which we were very thin given Craig's injury."

"We're also thin at singles because Doc is playing terrible. He looked so good at our first practice when he beat Billy and he played great in our first match of the season. It's been downhill ever since."

"Maybe this is the real Doc. Maybe the aberration was early in the year."

"No, I don't think that's it," I said. "Doc just hasn't been himself. He's a really low key guy, but he snapped at me for letting Craig continue his match. Something else is going on with him."

"Well, whatever it is, it makes Nate all the more valuable."

"Why didn't you ever mention him before?"

"Well, he has a downside. He's what I call an Excedrin player, a guy who can give you a headache." Lloyd went on to explain further. "Nate's one goal is to make it to Nationals. So, he waits for about a month into the regular season and joins whatever team he thinks gives him the best chance. In essence, he's a hired gun." Lloyd explained that when it comes to Nate, "It's all about him." If you try to tell Nate that there is no "I" in "team", he'd counter that there is one in "tennis".

I've seen this scenario in Hollywood sports movies. The beloved, protagonist team struggles in the beginning of the season, but then recruits some misfit player that turns their season around. So, why couldn't it work for me? Here's the bottom line. If we are going to compete with the juggernaut that is Union City, we had to have him.

After my conversation with Lloyd, I had a long phone discussion with Barry to bring him up to speed.

"We have enough players," Barry said in protest. "You've already added Gary and Steve. We need to get the guys who have been on the roster from the beginning more playing time, not less."

"Look, we need Nate if we are going to make a playoff run. And I want to try to make a playoff run."

"You're chasing a mirage. We're not going to make the playoffs."

"You don't know that," I said into the phone. "If we win all of our four remaining matches, we'll make it."

"You're setting expectations too high. There's no margin for error. It's like trying to win at love."

"What?" I asked, tilting my head toward the ceiling.

"You're putting too much pressure on yourself and the team. It's like trying to win every game with a love score. You're setting an impossible task and to try to reach it, you're justifying adding anyone to the roster, regardless of character. You said this guy can be a headache. We don't need that."

I paused a moment as this conversation was starting to give me a headache. "Barry, I wasn't calling you to ask you if we should add Nate. It was to inform you."

The phone went silent for moment. "Okay, you're the captain." There was another awkward silence before Barry said he had to go.

As soon as I got off the phone with Barry, I called Nate.

Hi Nate. This is Eric from the Albany tennis team. Did Lloyd tell you that I would call?

Yeah.

So, we'd really like you to join our team. We have a bunch of great guys on the...

Your record is only 3-2, right?

Yeah, but I think we can win our league with your help.

I don't want to just win the league. I want to go to Nationals.

That's our goal too. We have some really strong players.

Really? Your record is 3-2.

[Sigh]. How about you come out to practice and see for yourself?

The next day, Nate attended our Wednesday evening practice. He was about five foot eleven with a big, burly frame. I planned it so that he would play against Billy and Ross, two of our flashiest players. I partnered him with Matt, who had the strongest serve on the team. I was confident everything would go smoothly. I couldn't have been more wrong.

First, Nate opened his bag, pulled out six rackets, and spread them on the ground. I'm not sure if he was trying to impress or intimidate us with his array of rackets, which covered so much ground Ross tripped over one as he got off the bench.

Next, Nate complained about the tennis balls because it was not his preferred brand. Then, he complained that the warm-ups were taking too long. When the match started, he routinely complained to Matt, someone he met fifteen minutes ago, about his choice of where to stand on the court. I could feel my blood pressure rising every time Nate opened his mouth.

"This isn't going well," Barry said, shaking his head.

"It'll be okay," I said stubbornly.

Nate actually played great. He has a big serve and big ground strokes, but unfortunately also a big mouth. From a court away, I heard him ripping our public courts, saying they were much worse than what he was used to.

As our practice neared its end, a usually light hearted Mike asked in a serious tone, "Who's that guy and what's he doing here?"

"We're thinking of adding him."

Mike looked at me as if I was crazy. "Adding him to what? FBI's most wanted list?"

A couple of other players expressed similar sentiments and I realized I had a major decision to make. Nate, in person, proved to me that he's a top 4.0 tennis player. Unfortunately, he also proved to be a player that came with so much baggage he probably pays a surcharge when he flies.

Barry was now dead set against adding him although Lloyd still thought he was worth the risk. My heart told me that we had to have Nate if this team could reach its full potential. My brain told me Nate's addition would destroy my quest for stress-free matches. So, for the first time this year, I called my predecessor Dale to get his opinion. Dale has balanced being one of the most successful captains in Northern California without losing the respect of his players. After I explained the situation, he said, "Don't add him to your roster. It will screw up your team chemistry."

I had taken a lot of input from others (some solicited, some not) on the Nate situation. It was time for me to make a decision. As Lloyd put it, if it was tied two matches all in the league championship game and you had one doubles match left, would you want Nate out there or not? The answer was clearly yes. Still, I paused knowing Dale's advice. But, it's not Dale's team any more. It's mine. I had made my decision.

That night, I called Nate to invite him on the team. He again expressed concern about our 3-2 record, but said he trusted Lloyd's track record of being on winning teams and said he'd sign up. He also said he was going to be out of town for our next match against Richmond, but he would definitely make the match against Hayward.

As the outlook for my tennis team looked brighter, my relationship with Stacey was also improving. There is an old adage that says, "It is better to give than to receive." I proved that true on Friday. Knowing that Stacey had worked a lot of hours that week, I surprised her with flowers delivered to her work on Friday afternoon. Accompanying the flowers was a note, stating, "Our plans changed for tomorrow night. I bought two tickets for us to see Stormy Weather." Stormy Weather was a play she had mentioned in passing that she really wanted to see.

She called me Friday afternoon, ecstatic. "That was such a great surprise. Thanks so much. I was having a tough day, but this turned it around. Everyone in the office was jealous when the bouquet arrived..." She continued to talk with a lifted spirit and a tinge of admiration that I could be so spontaneously thoughtful. After the stress she had been under at work, just hearing her happy voice cleansed my soul. Yeah, it is better to give than to receive.

Richmond and League Rules

With a matchup against a very tough Hayward team looming, I had to make sure we didn't look past our next opponent, Richmond, who came into the match 0-5. The interesting thing about Richmond was their captain. Every captain has a different personality in this league, but I have been warned about Mikhail being a "handful".

We hosted Richmond on Saturday. Some of their players, who had paid large dues to be a member of their club, seemed annoyed that they had to play on our public courts, a far cry from the quality of the typical private club. As their players took the court, Mikhail grabbed a measuring tape out of his bag and measured the height of the net. He complained that the net was a ½ inch too high and demanded that we drop it. I felt like saying, "Look, your team is 0-5, does it really matter?", but instead, I lowered the net to his satisfaction. Then, he complained that the balls we supplied were too fuzzy.

When I tested the ball, it bounced fine and I concluded the only thing fuzzy was his logic. "You're welcome to open another can of your own if you like." He muttered something under his breath before he found something new to complain about, a few cracks on our public courts. During Mikhail's rant, my cell phone rang from inside my tennis bag.

As I jogged over to my bag, I looked back to see Mikhail's glare. He said to me, "You know, that would be our point if your cell had gone off during the match."

"Yes, I know," I said, turning my cell phone off and putting it back in my bag.

Due to Mikhail's shenanigans, we started about fifteen minutes late. After Gary and I won a hard fought first set in a tiebreaker against Mikhail, we had our next controversy. Mikhail is the kind of guy who would argue with a sign post. He spent the next five minutes disputing, incorrectly, whose serve it was and on what side the server should start in the next set.

This is exactly why every USTA captain should bring to each match The Code, which lists all of the USTA league rules and regulations. It's not enough to know the rules. When you have to deal with guys like Mikhail, you have to actually show him the rules in black and white.

After showing Mikhail the rule that proved him wrong, he mumbled, "They must have changed the rule recently." Yeah, right.

In the second set, we were up 5-4, with Mikhail serving to stay in the match. Four points into the game, Mikhail called out the score "40-15."

"No, no. The score is 30 all," I said, approaching the net. Gary nodded in agreement.

"No, it's 40-15," Mikhail said adamantly.

After a long argument and attempt to recall all of the points in the game, we could only remember three points, two they won and one we won. I said, "The rule in this case is that we play from 30-15, the specific points in the game we all agree on."

"No," Mikhail said, shaking his head. "As server, it's my call and I say the score is 40-15. That's the rule."

I respectfully asked him what he had been smoking and was it for medicinal purposes before pulling out the rule book again.

After showing him the relevant site proving my point, Mikhail grumbled under his breath that it *should* be the server's decision because he's the one that knows the score.

Mikhail went on to hold serve to knot the second set at five. Then, I started my next service game by sarcastically shouting the score "40 love". When Mikhail put both hands on his hips in clear protest, I said, "As server, it's my call." The congeniality went down from there.

I held my serve and then Gary and I broke Mikhail's partner to pull out a 7-6, 7-5 win. After the match, I learned Mikhail is one of those league players who always had an excuse for a loss. Here is a list of my favorite excuses, three of which Mikhail used, that all start with the quote, "I would've won if it wasn't for the…"

(1) Bad line calls
(2) Blinding sun (didn't your opponent have to deal with this too?)
(3) Wind (didn't your opponent have to… never mind)
(4) New racket (you believed the ad saying it would make you a better player)
(5) Play of my partner (Some people have never lost a doubles match… but their partners have)
(6) Heat, if temperatures were greater than 75 degrees
(7) Cold, if temperatures were less than 75 degrees
(8) Crowd noise (because you play your best tennis in libraries)
(9) Fact your opponent simply played better than you. The real reason for almost all defeats.

We ended up sweeping all five matches. Also winning that day was the reunited doubles team of Ross and Chris. Chris continued to develop more confidence and mental toughness. To be fair, one of his opponents was a weak player. His name was Victor, which was ironic since he had yet to win this year.

Victor would miss hit every fourth shot and after each time, he'd stare at his racket in disbelief. If he wanted to see the reason for his miss hits, he should have put a mirror on the throat of his racket.

It felt good to root for Ross and Chris. After having an early season goal to see them lose so I could break them up, I felt much better with the fact that I had become a Chris fan and sincerely hoped he would be mentally tough enough to make the playoff lineup. Today was another step toward that goal.

With our team win over Richmond, we improved our overall record to 4-2. Things were looking up and I no longer had those weird nightmares of radio talk show callers demanding that I be replaced.

After the match, we laughed and joked as a team over sandwiches and snacks. Several of the guys ripped Doc for bringing store-bought chili rather than his wife's homemade version. We were having so much fun talking that I lost track of the time.

I reached into my bag and grabbed my cell phone, which I had turned off. "Oh man!" I said, noticing the late hour and two missed phone calls from Stacey. By the time I raced home, showered and dressed, I was a half hour late meeting with Stacey to see the play, "Stormy Weather." Although we still made it to the play on time, the entire mood for the evening was ruined because we had to rush. It made for a few contentious moments and once again, my decision to captain the tennis team came under fire.

Hayward and Controversy

I had been looking forward to the Hayward match for some time, not just because the match had playoff ramifications, but because my parents were flying in for Father's Day weekend. I wanted to show my dad what a great job I'd done as captain of the Albany team.

Hayward came in with a 4-2 record in a three way tie for third place with Alameda and us. The Hayward captain, Gene, has earned quite a reputation. Shrewd and calculating, Gene is the best recruiter of any captain in our league. Although he has not had the number of championships that San Leandro captain Jeff has, he is just as committed to winning. Where Jeff believes in cultivating home grown talent and scouting competition, Gene believes in stretching the rules and recruiting ringers whether they live in his city or are flown in from a neighboring state. I heard he attends USTA 4.0 tennis tournament finals to recruit the winners. He's even been known to recruit players off Craig's List. Can you believe that? I would never have thought of that. Look on Craig's list for a used bike, yeah maybe. 4.0 tennis ringer, no.

I suspected Gene was up to his old tricks when the night before our match, a self rated player named Ming was added to his roster. The chances Gene would add a weak self rated player this late in the season was zero. Ming had to be a ringer. I added Steve and Nate earlier in the year so I shouldn't complain.

But when someone else does it, it makes you want to recite a speech about it hurting the integrity of the league. Soon, it becomes an arms race with every team trying to one up their competition. In essence, my logic is that it's okay for me to have a nuclear weapon, but the league is not safe with a nuclear weapon in Gene's sneaky hands.

On Wednesday, four days before our match, I got a phone call.

Hi. This is Gene from the Hayward tennis team. Is this Eric?

Yes, it is. I'm looking forward to our match on Sunday.

Yeah, about that. I just realized it's Father's Day this Sunday and I bet a lot of your players are busy that day. We should probably reschedule.

[My head was spinning. Normally, I'd be happy to re-schedule a match for a truly desperate captain, but this was different. First of all, we've had this match on the schedule for months and to the best of my knowledge, Father's Day has been scheduled for this day at least that long. Second of all, I'm sure he didn't call me because he was worried that *my* players couldn't make it.]

Actually, my players are fine and they've planned for it all season so I'd rather not change it now. Are you going to have trouble getting eight players?

Yeah, I am, seeing how it's Father's Day and all.

[I let out a sigh. Gene has 24 guys on his roster. I knew he wasn't having trouble getting eight guys. He was just having trouble getting his eight *best* guys.]

Well, just let me know if you think that you'll have to default any of the matches. No sense in my guys showing up for nothing, seeing how it's Father's Day and all. [My last comment was actually a test. If Gene had called me back to tell me he would be forfeiting matches, then I would have offered to reschedule. Not surprisingly, he never called back.]

I picked up my parents at the airport Friday evening. My parents, Stacey, and I had a great time in Napa Valley wine tasting on Saturday. Stacey had met my parents on many occasions. Although Stacey got along with both of my parents, she had bonded with my mom, often breaking away from my dad and me to talk about clothes, movies, or who knows what.

Late Saturday night, I retreated to my bedroom and listened to some meditation tapes that my dad brought up. I'm not sure if they really relaxed me, but I know it made my dad feel better that I listened to them. So, it was worth it.

On Sunday, my parents and Stacey accompanied me to the Albany courts at 10:00 AM. The weather was perfect, plenty of sunshine but a comfortable 80 degrees. I set them up in lawn chairs in front of the courts before I began to attend to my game day captain responsibilities.

When Gene arrived, he walked up to me muttering something about how he had to be away from his kids on "this sacred day". I chose not to respond and pointed him toward the warm-up court.

About twenty minutes before our match was scheduled to start, I stood, clipboard in hand, filling out the lineup card when a middle aged Asian man approached me. "Are you Gene?" he asked.

"Are you Ming?" I asked him. He nodded and, for a brief moment, I thought about saying, "Yes, I'm Gene. What are you doing here? Didn't you get my message saying we didn't need you this week? You might as well leave." Trust me, if Gene was in my place, he would have done it. Instead, I pointed toward court #3 where Gene was talking on his cell phone.

Gene, who had been a captain for many years, knew how to use the rules to his advantage. The league rules say you must default a match if a player arrives later than 15 minutes after the start time. Gene, his watch in hand, would call for a default exactly 15 minutes after the scheduled match start time, even if the player is running in from the parking lot. "Rules are rules. If we don't have them, then there's anarchy," he would say. It's stunts like this that earned him the nickname "Mean Gene." There's a rumor that he convinced a rookie, visiting captain that the home team can see a visiting team's lineup before making their own. "That's why they call it home court advantage," he supposedly said. Mean Gene had a knack of making strangers immediately.

Gene's Hayward team was built around their doubles. They had won almost every individual doubles match this year. Their Achilles' heel was singles. My guess is that Gene added Ming to be a singles ringer. That was confirmed when we exchanged lineups.

Gene had Ming at #1 singles. However, he was missing two of his top doubles players. I could tell immediately he had sacrificed his #1 doubles team, meaning he put his weakest team there. His strategy worked because that's where I placed Lloyd and Steve, our best doubles team.

As luck would have it, Gary and I were paired against Gene and his partner at #2 doubles. On the third point of the match, Gene smacked a first serve about six inches wide. Enraged, Gene shouted, "No way!" He walked over to our side of the court, placed a ball a foot inside the service box, and claimed, "That's where it landed."

Tennis is one of the few sports leagues where there are no officials. Players make the line calls on their side of the court. The only recourse is to call for a line judge from the spectators. However, that will only help for future calls.

Believing he had been wronged, Gene took matters into his own hands, engaging in a "makeup call" by calling one of our shots out that was actually clearly in. I simply let it go, but when he did it a second time, I asked as The Code recommends, "Are you sure?" In the over 300 league matches I have played, the answer to that question has always been, "Yes." I am still waiting for someone to say, "No, I'm not. But, I called it out hoping you wouldn't notice."

Gene responded curtly, "It was out."

I turned to Gene's partner. "How did you see it?"

This is the moment of truth. If a partner truly agrees with the "out" call, he will immediately say, "I saw the ball out."

If the partner actually saw it good, it is rare that he's brave enough to overrule his partner. However, most people don't want to lie. So, they immediately distance themselves without contradicting their partner by claiming that they didn't see. It's the "I saw nothing, I know nothing" defense. How could he not see it? What else would he be looking at?

On Gene's third bad call, I had had enough. "Let's get line judges out here."

Gene put his hands on his hips and looked at me as if I had insulted him. I turned to talk to Gary, refusing to even look in Gene's direction. As we waited for line judges, Gary's wife and two kids, ages four and two, arrived. The two kids raced to the fence, the older shouting, "Daddy! Uncle Eric!" and the younger saying, "Dad" and "Uncle". I walked over to the fence, bent down, and gave both high fives through the fence. At that point, a representative from each team entered the court to act as line judges. Gary's wife led both kids away from the fence and Gary and I refocused on tennis.

A line judge positioned themselves on each side of the net posts. They would call the lines on their side, but only if a player appealed a call. Gene proceeded to question every one of our calls that were remotely close, but neither line judge ever overruled us.

It was a close, intense match, probably the worse type for my father to have to endure. In the end, we lost 7-5, 7-6. When we shook hands at the net, I told Gene, "Nice match," before saying to myself, "Considering that you had to play without your seeing-eye dog."

Despite the loss, we came off the court to a hero's welcome. I was greeted with a kiss from Stacey and a pat on the back and a "good try" comment from my parents. Gary's two sons, caring very little about the tennis results, screamed for me to give them "airplane rides", which is a name I made up for picking them up and running around as they hold their arms out as if they were flying. "Okay," I said, picking up Gary's older son. "Better watch out for the turbulence," I added before shaking him as I jogged. As I ran by Stacey, I noticed her smiling broadly at the sight of me playing with Gary's son. I could see her recalculating in her mind an earlier date for us to get married and have a child.

After I gave out airplane rides to both kids, I found out that Lloyd and Steve slaughtered their doubles opponents 6-1, 6-1 in less than an hour. This meant the overall match was tied at one.

I sat down with my parents and Stacey to watch the final set at #1 singles. The match between Ming and Billy lasted well over two hours with Ming finally prevailing 6-4, 3-6, 7-5. It was Billy's first loss of the season. Everyone on our team was quick to congratulate The Kid on his extraordinary effort.

"You got another haircut," I said to Billy. "I hope you aren't like Samson where your hair is the source of your strength. Is this going to be your new look?"

"It will be for the summer. I start my internship at Craig's firm tomorrow."

"Congratulations. I'm proud of you," I said, which made Billy smile despite his loss.

Just a few minutes after Billy got off the court, Doc finished his match, easily winning at #2 singles. It was Doc's best played match in a while. This set up a winner take all match at #3 doubles. I remembered Lloyd's question to me. If it is two all, do you want Nate out there? I felt very comfortable having Nate and Mike team up against a strong Hayward team.

It didn't take long for controversy to occur and, surprisingly, it was fueled by Mike. One of the Hayward players was woefully foot faulting. I am not talking about a foot slightly on the baseline. I am talking about an entire leg crossing the baseline by more than a foot well before he struck the serve.

Mike came to the net and said, "I just want to tell you that you're foot faulting. Just be careful on that. I prefer not to call a line judge."

"Come on," the young Hayward player said. "This ain't the U.S. Open. It doesn't matter."

His captain, Gene, normally a stickler for the rules, did a 180 degree turn. "Your players are trying to win on a technicality."

I'm not sure how following a basic tennis rule qualifies as a technicality, but I chose to ignore Gene. Mike normally deals with tense situations with humor. When it was Mike's turn to serve, he walked all the way up to the service line, which is half way into the court between the net and the baseline and smacked an ace past a confused opponent.

"What are you doing?" his opponent asked. "You can't serve from there."

"Why not?" Mike asked.

"Because the rules say you have to serve from behind the baseline."

"Exactly my point," Mike said. "Now that we agree on the rule, let's get line judges out here to call for foot faults." Nate laughed hysterically before giving Mike a high five.

"Are all your matches this contentious?" my dad asked, sitting next to me.

"No, just this one," I said, beginning to feel a slight pain in the pit of my stomach.

Sensing my discomfort, Stacey rubbed my back as she asked, "Are you okay?"

"I'm fine," I said, telling a half-truth. I offered a fake smile which I am sure she saw through.

The match resumed with line judges and, thanks in part to some fantastic play by Nate, we pulled out the first set 6-3. Things changed drastically in the second set. The united front that Nate and Mike had built as a result of the arguments with the Hayward team disappeared. The Hayward team started to pick up their play and Nate began to turn on Mike.

Nate complained, loud enough for everyone to hear, that Mike shouldn't lob so much. Then, he complained that he needed to come to the net more. "That's not the way you play tennis!" he exclaimed when they lost at set point.

Between the second and third set is one of the rare times coaching is allowed during a league match. I left Stacey and my parents to try to settle down our guys. Nate sat on the bench while Mike stood about forty feet away, leaning on the fence. I walked over to Mike. Before I could say anything, Mike said, "I cannot play with that guy. I'm not going to have some young punk tell me how to play the game."

"Who you calling a punk?" Nate said, rising from his bench and approaching Mike.

"That would be you," Mike said, standing his ground.

Before I could intervene, Nate shoved Mike, who staggered back a few steps.

I immediately stepped in between the two and shouted at Nate, "Hey! Calm down."

"No one talks to me like that," Nate said.

As I tried to compose Nate, I noticed Mike had grabbed his tennis bag and started walking off the court. I raced over to him. "What are you doing?"

"I'm quitting. I can't play with that guy."

"Mike," I said, walking alongside him as I could feel my heart beating rapidly. "The overall match is tied two all. You're not walking out on Nate. You're walking out on the team."

With that, Mike stopped to glare at me. "Will you tell him not to say one word about my play in the third set? Not one word."

"Yes."

"If he does, I swear I'll walk out."

"It's a deal," I said, leading Mike back on the court. I walked over to Nate to play peacemaker. "Listen, Mike can be a little sensitive on the court. Can you just not talk about his play? You're showing him up in front of everybody."

"I'm just trying to help the guy out," Nate said, holding his arms away from his body.

"Just promise you won't say anything to him the rest of the match."

"Fine."

With that, I headed back to the sidelines where I was greeted harshly by Doc. "Why is this Nate guy even on the team?"

I folded my arms in front of my chest as I turned to look back on the courts. "It's just a little spat. They'll work it out."

"No, they won't," Doc said. "You better step up and do something."

As Doc walked away from me and toward our other Albany teammates, my mom approached me. "Stacey is going to drive us back to your house. This is very hard for your dad to watch. We should really go."

"Okay," I said, a little disappointed. "I'll be home in about an hour."

I waved goodbye to my dad who was already halfway to the parking lot. I felt bad. He came to see a tennis match, not a bad episode of the Jerry Springer Show. Maybe it was a good thing my dad did not stay. The final set was one of the most difficult spectacles of tennis I have ever had to watch. Nate and Mike had far more talent, but they were not playing as a team: just two individual players who happen to be on the same side of the net. They did not communicate. Nate kept his promise and said nothing verbally. However, his body language spoke volumes any time Mike would miss a shot. Nick's slumped shoulders and head shaking seemed to shout, "I can't believe you missed that shot! My invalid grandmother could have made that shot with her eyes closed."

The Albany crowd could sense the tense situation on the court and did not know how to react at times. In the end, it was the few Hayward supporters who were most vocal as we fell 6-4 in the final set.

Nate stormed off the court, with nothing to say to me or other team members. Mike, on the other hand, walked directly to me. "No one puts their hands on me. I'm not going to play on the same team with that guy. So, you have a roster decision to make, captain. It's either me or him."

Mike didn't wait around to hear me respond. Still stunned, I watched him walk away before I could say a word. Lost in all of the drama, we had lost the overall match 3-2, snapping a three match win streak and dropping our overall record to 4-3.

That afternoon, I drove my parents to the airport. I was too embarrassed with the fiasco that masqueraded as a tennis match to even talk about it with my dad. I feared what he witnessed would only confirm his initial concerns of me taking over as captain. Furthermore, the pain in my stomach had worsened, but I didn't dare mention it to my parents.

After I dropped my parents off at the airport, I drove to Stacey's house with plans to spend some alone time with her. However, as soon as I arrived, all I could manage was a quick kiss before crashing on the bed.

"What's going on with you?"

"My stomach, it hurts again," I said, curling up in a ball on the bed.

"What can I do?"

"Just lie down with me."

"I really need to finish this memo," Stacey said, gesturing toward her laptop. "I need it for my meeting tomorrow morning."

"Come on," I said, motioning with my hand. "Just for a few minutes."

Stacey relented and laid down on the bed, wrapping her arms around me. I dozed off for what seemed like a few minutes before awaking to strong stomach cramps. "Ow! This is bad."

"That's it," Stacey said, sitting up. "We're going to the hospital."

"What about your work?"

"I can do it when we get back from the hospital. Let's go."

She loaded me into her car and drove to the emergency room, where I waited for over an hour behind more serious cases. It was nice to have Stacey with me to keep me company and be present as a source of support. I finally saw a doctor who ran a series of tests before concluding that I had something he referred to as "Nervous Stomach". He explained that the brain releases a lot more acids into the stomach when you are stressed, which could cause my symptoms of abdominal pain and constipation.

"Most importantly," the doctor said. "I want you to try to learn to cope with stress better. Please go back to the classes that the clinic offers."

The doctor prescribed medication designed to flush my system and put me on a specific diet over the next couple of days. I purchased a blood pressure kit so I could monitor it any time I wanted.

By the time I got home at eight thirty, I was exhausted. While Stacey made some soup, I snuck upstairs to get on the computer to see the other weekend results. The juggernaut that is Union City crushed San Leandro, sweeping them 5-0. Terry, San Leandro's best singles player who missed our match earlier this season, actually took a set from Union City's ringer Ace. But, Ace prevailed in three sets. Even San Leandro's topspin-loving Chang twins fell in two tough sets against Union City's # 1 doubles team. Union City was a perfect 7-0 on the season without dropping a single individual match. Incredible.

Here are the standings after seven games of the regular season:

1. Union City   7-0   [35]
2. San Leandro 6-1   [25]
3. Alameda   5-2   [24]
4. Hayward   5-2   [22]
5. Albany   4-3   [21]
6. Berkeley   3-4   [17]
7. Piedmont   3-4   [14]
8. Oakland   1-6   [8]
9. Richmond   1-6   [8]
10. Hercules   0-7   [1]

With two matches left in the regular season, it had become a four team race to claim the final three playoff spots. We had slipped to fifth place and a sad realization hit me. We no longer controlled our own destiny to make the playoffs. We had to beat Piedmont and Oakland, two relative lightweights left on our schedule, but we needed Alameda or Hayward to lose. It appeared possible with Alameda still having to play both Union City and San Leandro while Hayward still had San Leandro and winless Hercules on their schedule.

"What are you doing?" Stacey asked in disbelief with a bowl of soup in her hand. "You're on that tennis website again. I swear you're addicted. I thought you were in bed."

"I'm going," I said, shutting down my computer. Like a prison guard, Stacey escorted me to my room. I sat down on my bed and she maneuvered a tray of soup in front of me. I had a few sips. "That's enough for now," I said, lying back in my bed. "I think I'm going to get some sleep."

"Okay, I'm going to leave, but you're going to have to promise me that you're not going back on the computer."

"Promise," I said, holding my right arm up.

"Call me if you need anything," Stacey said before giving me a goodbye kiss. I would have preferred she stay and lay with me in bed, but I knew she had work to do. Between wine tasting, my tennis match, and our unexpected trip to the hospital, I had monopolized most of her weekend.

As I watched her leave, I felt so lucky to have her in my life. I loved her and couldn't imagine life without her. Sitting on my bed staring at the walls, I forced myself to address the issue I was avoiding: Nate. I wanted to believe things could only get better with Nate. The worse had to be behind me, but even I would not be able to talk myself out of what I knew I had to do. I didn't take any further counsel before I picked up the phone next to the bed to give him the news. In the end, it would be a good move for my emotional health. I practiced what I would say. The exact quote was, "I don't think you're the right fit for our team." Sounds like something a recruiting manager would say after interviewing a bad candidate.

"What are you talking about?" Nate asked, sounding shocked.

"You were too vocal on the court today and it rubbed a lot of guys the wrong way. Then, you shoved Mike. I just think it's best we part ways. I can refund your team registration fee if you like."

There was a long pause as I think Nate was still processing what I was telling him. Finally, he responded with the equivalent of "You can't fire me because I quit", immediately telling me that he would play for a San Francisco team in another league because they were much better. The last thing that Nate said to me was, "Your team sucks and you can kiss the playoffs goodbye. I want to play with winners."

As I hung up the phone, I laid down in my bed. That was a lot of work and a lot of unnecessary tension to accomplish absolutely nothing. I should have followed Dale's advice not to add Nate to the team. It turns out real life is nothing like those Hollywood movies. Still, I felt an emotional weight was lifted with Nate's departure. I quickly fell into a peaceful sleep as I listened to my dad's meditation tapes.

Piedmont and Surviving the Storm

I took off work Monday and Tuesday. By Tuesday afternoon, I began to feel much better. That evening, I sent an email to the team stating that Nate and I came to a mutual decision that he was going to play for another team in San Francisco. I received many email replies. Here are a few samples: "addition by subtraction", "our gain is San Francisco's loss", "thank God".

We had an excellent practice this week. I didn't feel 100% yet, so I watched from the sidelines. With Nate nowhere to be found, the tone of the practice was relaxed and pleasant. It was also jovial, for another reason. Craig was there and played tennis for the first time since his injury earlier in the season.

"How's the leg doing?" I asked him midway through practice.

"Great," Craig said, smiling from ear to ear.

At the end of practice, Mike, of all people, called a meeting and we all gathered in a circle. Looking at Craig, Mike said, "I'm going to keep this short. A bunch of us chipped in and bought you a 'Welcome Back' present." Al handed Craig a 24 pack of bottled water. "Try drinking some of it when you play tennis." I looked around and saw the smiles and heard the laughter. For better or worse, these were the guys with whom I wanted to try to win a league championship. No matter how it would come out, I would be proud to be their captain.

Just as I became content with the status of the team, the status of my relationship with Stacey took a turn for the worse. I knew it when on Thursday night, she said, "We need to talk." In the history of all relationships, nothing ever good came out of conversations that start with, "We need to talk."

Stacey went on to say, "I've watched you captain this tennis team. You're so emotionally invested in its success. I mean you live and die with the results of each match. Why?"

I paused for a moment wondering where this was going. "I'm doing it for the guys on the team."

"Nah," Stacey said, shaking her head. "I've been to the matches and the rest of the guys aren't nearly as obsessed as you. None of them take the losses as hard as you do. None of them are making themselves sick. You entered this season with doubts and fears as to whether you would be a good captain. Yet, you took it on and you continue to work so hard at trying to be the best captain ever."

Speechless, I stared at her for a while and watched as she shifted in her seat. "This isn't about tennis," I finally said. "What's this really about?"

"It's about us, our relationship. The fact is that you have doubts and fears about being a father. If you valued our relationship as much as you did this tennis team, we'd be married with kids."

"You can't compare becoming a father for a lifetime to captaining a tennis team for a season. I love you with all my heart, but right now I'm not sure I want kids."

"How can you say that?" Stacey asked, leaning forward. "I see you around Gary's kids. You're great."

"It's not the same. I see them once every two weeks. I'm not sure I want the responsibility of being an everyday parent."

"Well, I do and I want you to have the courage to take on the responsibility, like you did with the tennis team."

"Is that what this is about? You're upset that I took on this role of captain. Do you want me to quit?"

Stacey shook her head. "I don't want you to care about your tennis team less. I want you to care about our relationship more."

It was an excruciatingly difficult conversation. At the end of it, we agreed to take a month break so I could determine what I wanted from the relationship. As dictated by Stacey, the status quo was no longer an option. She wanted to be married with children.

As I went to bed that night, I felt terrified at the notion of losing Stacey. I loved our relationship and I loved her. I always had a picture in my mind of us married, although I did not like the fact that she was now trying to pressure me into it.

The one thing Stacey has made clear: she wanted kids. I felt I owed it to her to be honest. The simple truth is the picture in my mind with us happily married never included any kids.

Motivated and focused, our team met at our courts on Sunday and carpooled as a team to Piedmont. It was a must win match for both teams. There are two types of teams that are dangerous to play. There's the ridiculously talented, like Union City, but the other type is less obvious: the desperate. Piedmont was a desperate team, having a small glimmer of a chance to make the playoffs. They would either give up, taking the opportunity to play some of their weaker players, or go for it with their top lineup. Once we exchanged lineups, I realized they did the latter.

Craig, playing at #2 singles, again brought his son to the match. As Craig battled on the court, his son spent more time texting than watching his father. Keeping hydrated throughout the match, Craig won in straight sets to give us the first win of the day. He still had enough energy to go back on the courts and hit with his son. Ever since his son told him how fun it was to play tennis on video game Wii, Craig has made it his life's mission to make his son play the real thing.

My stomach had greatly improved and I felt well enough to play. Gary and I, who love to serve and volley, played two seniors at #1 doubles. Our opponents played smart, keeping us off balance with offensive lobs. We lost the first set 6-3. It was a key moment. It's the biggest difference between a good doubles team and a great one: the ability to adjust strategies and tactics. I have seen many teams that lose the first set, make absolutely no changes, and proceed to, surprise, surprise, lose the next set.

In the second set, Gary and I took a few steps back from the net. Instead of defensively hitting overheads as we back pedaled and surrendered the net, we were hitting overhead winners. On one overhead, I smacked it right at one of our opponents at the net. Instinctively, I raised my hands and apologized. It is a quirky thing. All tennis players with any sportsmanship apologize, but no one really means it. Want proof? On the very next point, if they get a short lob, they'll do it again.

Tennis players are just strange. Can you imagine a football player putting a good hit on a receiver and then apologizing?

After making our adjustments, we came back to take the second set 6-2. With all five matches going at once, I found out between the second and third set that we split the other four matches. So, likely our season was going to come down to our match. Every one of our players stayed to cheer us on. Playing in the deciding third set is much easier than watching. Gary and I remained focused, attacked their weaker backhands, and pressed the issue at the net. We won the final set 6-1 to take the overall match 3-2.

We celebrated our big win as we enjoyed the Piedmont-provided lunch that included hot pulled pork sandwiches, coleslaw, chips and drinks. Doc, who played great today in his win, pulled me aside to say, "I know I haven't played well lately. I appreciate you sticking with me."

"You're my guy," I said, slapping him on the shoulder.

"My wife and I have had some issues in our marriage," Doc said. "But, we're working them out. That's big because it was affecting my focus in matches."

Doc's comments hit me like a ton of bricks and I was reminded once again that as captain I was not playing with a deck of cards, but with real people who were going through real emotions. Her absence and the absence of her famous chili at our matches made sense now. "I had no idea, but I'm glad you're working them out."

"Yep, relationships can be tough, especially when the two parties want different things."

I nodded my head as I thought about Stacey. "I know what you mean."

It wasn't until that night that I realized exactly where we stood in the playoff race. We received some help from Union City when they beat Alameda 4-1. Maybe Union City captain Pablo really is my friend. Alameda handed Union City their first loss in an individual doubles match. Meanwhile, Union City's singles stars Ace and Brian spanked Alameda's two eighteen year old kids in straight sets.

We received additional help from San Leandro as they knocked off Hayward 3-2. Despite getting a lot of help this week, we still did not control our own destiny. I wish we would have won one more individual match today against Piedmont. Heck, I wish we would have won just one more individual match at any point this year.

Here are the standings after eight weeks:

1. Union City   8-0   [39]

2. San Leandro 7-1   [28]
3. Alameda   5-3   [25]
4. Hayward   5-3   [24]
5. Albany   5-3   [24]
6. Berkeley   4-4   [20]
7. Piedmont   3-5   [16]
8. Richmond   2-6   [13]
9. Oakland   1-7   [10]
10. Hercules   0-8   [1]

As it stood, if we ended in a tie in win-loss record and individual matches won, we would lose out to both Alameda and Hayward because we had lost more individual sets.

Here are the key matches for the final week of the regular season: Albany at Oakland, Hercules at Hayward, and Alameda at San Leandro.

I knew Hayward would sweep Hercules 5-0, so that meant we couldn't catch Hayward. So, our only hope to make the playoffs was for Alameda to lose at least two individual matches to San Leandro and we would have to beat Oakland 5-0.

Here's the problem. San Leandro is already locked into second place and they have absolutely nothing to play for. San Leandro captain Jeff might just play his second tier guys and take some perverse joy in knocking us out, by losing. In fact, if he believes that Alameda would be an easier first round playoff match-up, he probably would throw the match. I began to get a headache. Our playoff lives were dependent on the help of either our arch rival who had no incentive to win or "0 for the season" Hercules.

Our last regular season practice on Wednesday evening was a good one, even though everyone knew if things did not work out this weekend it would be the last practice of the year.

After practice, Matt and I decided to grab dinner at a local Italian restaurant. "It's been a great season," Matt said as our dinner arrived at the table. His comment suggested he felt the season was coming to an end.

"Well, hopefully we can extend the season a bit longer, but we have to win this Friday night."

"Yeah, sorry I won't be able to make it," Matt said, taking his first bite of his ravioli. "The rehearsal dinner is Friday night and I might be missed."

"And then the big day is Saturday," I said with a smile. "Are you nervous?"

Matt shook his head. "Nah, getting married is easy. Planning a wedding, that's what's hard. And we're finally done with that."

"You two have been dating for three years. How did you know it was time?"

"She told me," Matt said with a laugh.

"Seriously, how'd you know?"

Matt put down his fork, finished chewing, and looked me straight in the eye. "Okay, I'll be serious. After six months of dating, I knew I wanted to spend the rest of my life with her. I wanted to have a family with her. It was just a matter of timing. As soon as I had my finances in order, I proposed." Matt's forehead wrinkled. "Why do you ask?"

"Well, Stacey and I have been dating for three years and she has done more than hint that she's ready for marriage and kids."

"Oooh. Well, the question is, 'Are you ready?'"

"Hey, I love Stacey and I don't want to lose her."

Matt leaned closer to me. "That's not what I asked. I asked whether you were ready."

"For marriage and kids? Honestly... I don't know. That's why I was asking about your situation."

"Well, if she has been mentioning being married with children, you better figure out what you want... and quick."

On Thursday, the landscape of the East Bay league completely changed. The USTA disqualified Union City's star self-rated singles player Ace, meaning he was retroactively moved up to 4.5 as of the beginning of the season. This means all of his five wins this year would automatically be turned into losses. Since Ace played against Alameda and us, it gave us one more win, but Hayward's individual match win total remained unchanged.

Here are the new standings:

1. Union City   8-0   [34]
2. San Leandro 7-1   [29]
3. Alameda   5-3   [26]
4. Albany   5-3   [25]
5. Hayward   5-3   [24]
6. Berkeley   4-4   [21]
7. Piedmont   3-5   [17]
8. Richmond   2-6   [13]
9. Oakland   1-7   [10]
10. Hercules   0-8   [1]

As a self-rated player, Ace was subject to USTA disqualification procedures if his match scores, considering his opponent's strength, did not align with his rating level. The USTA computer made the final decision after Ace's latest thumping of Alameda's talented eighteen year old singles player.

Thus, Ace's DQ actually gave us control of our playoff destiny. Now, we were ahead of Hayward and if we could beat Oakland 5-0, we would qualify for the playoffs.

Oakland and Discovering a Conspiracy

With only one more game left in the regular season, we were on the verge of achieving a once unfathomable goal- a playoff berth. We played on Friday evening at a luxurious club in the hills of Oakland. I had a strong lineup with Billy and Doc at singles and Lloyd and Steve, Gary and me, and Ross and Chris at doubles.

I was confident that we would win all five matches, especially when I noticed Doc's wife present. Her presence had to be a good sign for their marriage which likely would correlate to more focused, better play from Doc. Furthermore, Oakland had weak singles and only one strong doubles team, which had accounted for five of the team's ten individual match wins of the year. Every time, they played their strong team at #1 doubles so I played Lloyd and Steve at #1 expecting them to be able to handle them.

I had been friendly with Manny, the Oakland captain, for years. He was a nice guy who played by the rules. Our teams had a very friendly rivalry over the past five years.

After we exchanged lineups, I was shocked. "What are you doing putting your best doubles team at #3 doubles?"

"I've been given a mission," Manny said with a smile. "To get one individual match win today."

"A mission?"

"The Hayward captain Gene promised to host our entire team at his restaurant if we get one individual win."

I shook my head, wondering if I should detest or admire Gene. This gives new meaning to the phrase, "Winner, winner, chicken dinner!"

"So, you were part of this conspiracy?"

"Hey," Manny said, holding his arms out defensively. "Gene was offering to pay to add guys to our roster that he made contact with on Craig's List. But, I told him no. If we were going to beat you, it would be with our guys."

So, the challenge was on. Not surprising, we won in straight sets in both singles and at #1 and #2 doubles. The entire team gathered on the deck overlooking the courts to watch Ross and Chris. Everyone knew that if Ross and Chris won, we would officially qualify for the playoffs.

Ross and Chris, both just shy of six feet, were dwarfed by their opponents. A good three inches taller, the Oakland tandem hit with power. What they lacked was consistency. If Ross and Chris could keep a rally going for a few shots, one of the Oakland giants would likely smash a ball into the net or long. One of the Oakland guys was left handed and the other right handed.

By the time I completed my match, Ross and Chris had won the first set 6-2, and were up in the second set 4-3. The sun began to set and the Oakland club's lights turned on. From our perch on the deck overlooking the courts, all of the players from both teams gathered to watch the match while enjoying chicken wings.

Farther down the deck, watching by himself, was none other than Jeff, the San Leandro captain. I barely recognized him without shades. Wearing his trademark black baseball cap, he

quietly watched the match. I decided not to go over to him.
"Come on Ross. Come on Chris. Let's go!" I shouted after the
Oakland team held serve to even the second set at four.

I grabbed a beer and stood in between Lloyd and Gary. In
the past, I would watch matches alone and agonize over the
result. I think I considered the result would be a clear reflection
upon me as a captain. I have changed my outlook and it is much
healthier. I watched side by side with my teammates because we
were all in this together. Plus, the camaraderie of my teammates
made the tense situation a lot more enjoyable.

At 4-4, Chris smoked a forehand passing shot that appeared
to hit the line, but his opponent called it out. As Ross and Chris
put both hands on top of their heads in disbelief, I noticed it was
getting darker and cooler. A light wind began to pick up and I
put on a long sleeve sweatshirt. The Oakland duo broke Chris'
serve and then held to take the second set 6-4.

I took advantage of the rule allowing coaching between the
second and third full sets. I walked down to the courts to talk to
Ross and Chris, feeling the cool, crisp air against my face.
Coaching during a match is an art. Sometimes, a captain can
screw his players up more than help. In fact, if my players lose
the first set and win the second, I say very little, figuring that
they are on a roll. However, in this case, I was worried that the
match might be slipping away.

"Did everyone else win?" Ross asked before I could even
say anything.

"Yeah."

"I can't believe we blew that second set," a sweat-drenched
Chris said, looking down at the ground.

"Hey," I said. "You can't worry about the past. Focus on
the present. Just pick yourselves up, dust yourselves off, and
come out stronger than ever in the third set. You can do it. You
guys are better than this team." I knelt down to get at eye level

with the sitting Ross and Chris. "What do you guys think happened from the first set to the second?"

"We didn't return serve as well," Ross said before drinking Gatorade.

"Yeah, I noticed that," I said. "You just have to get into rallies. They will make mistakes. If need be, pull your partner back to the baseline on first serves."

"Did you see anything else we should do?" Ross asked.

"Yeah," I said, slapping Chris on the shoulder to make sure he was listening. It was important for Chris' nerves that he focus on specific game plan. When you have a specific task that you need to accomplish, you don't waste time being nervous. "Okay, this is a righty-lefty combination. They are playing with their backhands down the middle. You should be hitting every shot down the middle. Got it?"

"Got it," Chris said nodding.

Hitting toward the middle of the court (when both opponents are at the net or on the baseline) is a winning strategy for the following reasons: First, it cuts down on the angles that your opponents can hit. Second, you take advantage of the lowest part of the net. Third, you eliminate the chance you will inadvertently miss wide. And fourth, an opponent may hesitate thinking it's his partner's ball to hit.

"Okay, go get 'em," I said before I pumped my fist and left.

My pep talk appeared to work as Ross held his serve at love to take a 1-0 lead. I leaned on the deck railing with clasped hands and practiced my deep breathing exercises to help me relax.

Ross and Chris executed the game plan perfectly, blasting low shots up the middle. The set lasted a mere twenty minutes as our guys won 6-1. Chris closed the match out with an ace. A big roar came from the deck as our team celebrated with high fives. A few of the guys acted like they would dump the ice chest on top of me. On this cold night, I threatened to kick them off the team if they did it.

As the team raced down the courts to congratulate Ross and Chris, Jeff walked over to me, shook my hand, and said, "Congratulations." It's funny how I can perceive such a sentiment as sounding fake coming from Jeff. It felt like he was saying, "Congratulations on beating a 1-8 team today. Good for you and your little team."

"Thanks," I said, forcing myself to smile.

"You're in the playoffs now," Jeff said, which came as no surprise that he had done his homework and knew today's stakes. "We look forward to playing you in the first round."

"Not so fast," I said, with raised eyebrows. "That will only happen if you beat Alameda this weekend."

"Like I said," Jeff said with a smirk. "We look forward to playing you."

I paused a moment to think and couldn't help speaking my mind. "So, you're in the position where you can pick your first round opponent. You must want to play us."

"Yep, we do," Jeff said nodding. "I'll be in touch with the day and time of our match on Monday."

Jeff turned to leave and my mind raced. Was he going to make sure he played us in the first round to exact his revenge from last year? Or did he believe we were an easier matchup than Alameda, the team he was sure he would beat? Either way, I am sure he felt confident that he could beat us. I remember, earlier this year, that he bragged how he beat us without his best players. Who knows? Maybe Mean Gene from Hayward bribed him with free dinners.

I called my dad to tell him the news. "Congratulations," he said. "I know how hard you worked."

I could tell my dad was genuinely happy for me, but it still bothered me that the only match he witnessed was our loss to Hayward where the team imploded. I really wanted him to have another image of my reign as captain, but I didn't dare suggest that he travel back up for the playoffs. "Dad, my chief goal was to make the playoffs, but now that I'm there, I would love to upset San Leandro. Then, I would have matched what Dale did last year."

"Are you competing with Dale?" my dad asked.

The question stunned me because I never thought about it like that. "No, I'm just trying to earn my players respect and I feel like I'll always be measured by what Dale accomplished."

My dad paused a minute to tap his fingers. "Don't look outward for acceptance. It's your own standards that count. If you're happy with how you and the team have done, that's all that counts."

I thought about what my dad said throughout the weekend. At the end of the weekend, I logged onto the USTA website Sunday evening to check the results. True to his word, San Leandro crushed Alameda 4-1 and Hayward swept hapless Hercules 5-0. This left the following year end standings and playoffs seedings.

1. Union City   9-0   [39]
2. San Leandro 8-1   [33]
3. Albany   6-3   [30]
4. Hayward   6-3   [29]
5. Alameda   5-4   [27]
6. Berkeley   5-4   [24]
7. Piedmont   3-6   [17]
8. Richmond   2-7   [15]
9. Oakland   1-8   [10]
10. Hercules   0-9   [1]

This meant the local playoffs would see...
#1 seed Union City hosts #4 seed Hayward, and
#2 seed San Leandro hosts #3 seed Albany.

Local Playoffs and a New Level of Pressure

Across the Northern California section, there were 253 Adult 4.0 teams that registered and competed during the regular season. 64 teams qualified for the local playoffs, which is the USTA's answer to NCAA's March madness. In the span of just two weekends, the surviving number shrinks to a sweet sixteen that advance to the District Championships.

There's a new kind of pressure when you get to the playoffs. You have to win or your season is over. It's that simple. As captain, you go through the painstaking torture of second and third guessing yourself about the lineup. Then, for the remaining portion of the week you worry that everyone stays healthy for the big match.

I announced the lineup at our Wednesday night practice. The players left out of the lineup were all okay with my decision and each said they would come to the match to support the team. After practice, I said goodbye to Barry, who was leaving for a two week European vacation for his wedding anniversary.

"Don't forget to have fun and enjoy the experience," Barry said to me. "No matter what happens, you've done a great job just getting to the playoffs."

"Thanks," I said. "You've been a big help."

On match day, we gathered as a team at the Albany courts and made the thirty minute drive to San Leandro. It gave me peace of mind to go down together so I knew where everyone was. It was going to be a warm day as we would play on an early July afternoon.

When we arrived at the match, Jeff greeted each of my players personally, saying, "Hi, I'm Jeff. And you are?" Sounds like a friendly gesture, but in actuality he was just trying to figure out exactly who was there. He probably had a notebook full of scouting reports on each of our players.

I sat down next to Lloyd on a bench as we made the final decision on what positions to place the players in the lineup. All year I had been playing Billy at #1 singles and Doc at #2 singles, mostly due to Billy's band practice. I figured Jeff had to notice that. I wanted to sacrifice Doc to San Leandro's star singles player Terry. So, I was playing for a split in singles and hoped we could somehow pull out two doubles. In doubles, I put Lloyd and Steve at #1, Ross and Matt at #2, and Gary and me at #3.

Lloyd nodded his approval with the lineup and I walked over to Jeff, who was all business. "Ready to exchange?" he asked, dipping his head.

I nodded and we exchanged lineup cards. "Yes!" I exclaimed to myself. I had guessed right in singles.

Jeff, unfazed, barked out the court assignments. All five matches would be going on at once. I had a short meeting to give a rough scouting report of San Leandro's players. For the first time this year, I asked everyone to stick their hands in the middle of a circle. "Albany on three. One, two, three..." Everyone shouted, "Albany!"

Gary and I took the courts against two tough opponents who apparently were seasoned 4.0 tournament players. Both were strong, athletic guys who played aggressive, power tennis. It took a set for Gary and me to get accustomed to their big serves. After dropping the first set, we came back to win the second set to force a full third set.

Local Playoffs and a New Level of Pressure

At the break before the third set, I got some extra water and found out that we split the singles matches. San Leandro's best singles player, Terry, easily dispatched Doc 6-3, 6-3 while Billy prevailed in two tough sets 6-4, 6-4. The other two matches were still going on. Ross and Matt were in the middle of their third set while Lloyd and Steve were down a set and just beginning a second set tiebreak.

In the middle of the second game of our third set, a big applause mixed in with some hooting and hollering came from the San Leandro crowd. They were reacting to their doubles team, the Chang twins, beating Lloyd and Steve two courts over. We were now down 1-2 in the overall match. About ten minutes later, we received some good news, Ross and Matt, in the court right next to us, came back to pull out their match 6-4 in their final set.

At this point, the entire crowd began to assemble behind our court with the overall match tied at two. In our match, with both teams serving well with no service breaks, the final set went to tiebreak. The first team to get to seven, winning by two, would take the match.

Playing flawless tennis in the tiebreak, we took a 6-3 lead. I would get to serve the next two points. "We got this," Gary said encouragingly as we walked to the baseline. "You get to be the hero," he said before heading back toward the net. I took a deep breath, knowing my doubles match, the overall playoff match, and the entire season hung in the balance. I let the importance of the moment fade and I focused on serving to the returner's backhand. I placed my first serve perfectly, but hit my half volley right into the net when it was returned hard and low at my ankles. I caught a quick glimpse of our opponents who gave each other a low five. Frustrated, I yanked the ball off the ground.

"Don't worry about it," Gary said, greeting me. "We're still up 6-4. Just get the serve in and I'll take care of the rest." Gary ended his speech with a slap on the back. I nodded as I walked back alone to the baseline to serve from the deuce court.

I wiped some sweat from my forehead before bouncing the ball methodically as I readied myself to serve. I pounded the ball over the net and straight to my opponent's backhand.

"Long!" yelled our opponent as I winced, unsure of the accuracy of the call. As I walked back to serve, I could hear someone say, "Come on, Eric" from the other side of the fence. When I turned around to face my opposition, I noticed the service returner had inched in from his previous position. I tossed the ball, smacking it at its apex, and raced toward the net. As I took a few steps, I could tell my serve was going to go meekly toward the serve returner's forehand.

The service return was crushed, low and cross court. I bent down as I readied myself to hit a defensive, backhand volley. But, it never came. It never got to me. With great instinct and an unbelievable will to poach, Gary volleyed the ball crisply, splitting the two opponents for a winner.

The Albany contingent erupted and raced on to the court. After we shook hands with our opponents, Gary and I were mobbed by our teammates. It was one of the best moments of my entire sports life. We had upset San Leandro… again!

On Sunday, still on a high from Saturday's victory, I made the trek down to Union City to watch their playoff match against Hayward. I got there at 11:45, fifteen minutes before the match was supposed to start. There was already a large contingent of fans. In addition to the small grandstand, people had folding lounge chairs lined up along the three courts.

I located Pablo, Union City's captain, who was looking at the five Hayward players warming up on the courts. I recognized Ming, Hayward's self-rated Craig's list ringer, and of course their captain, Mean Gene. It appeared that Hayward only had five players present. Even though there were plenty of courts, Union City had opted to play only three matches at noon, with the final two coming on afterward.

I sat down on a folding chair that I brought and hoped I would go unnoticed. A few minutes later, I watched Gene exit the courts and approach Pablo to exchange lineups. When the teams took the courts for the match, I noticed that Ming was playing against a middle aged man that I did not recognize. I later learned that his name is Calvin when the crowd repeatedly shouted it. So, Pablo must have held back Brian, who had been warming up earlier, to play at #2 singles. On the other two courts, Union City played their two best doubles teams, the same guys who trounced us in our regular season match.

"Hey there. Are you here to scout, my friend?" Pablo said, greeting me with a handshake.

"Maybe, a little," I said with a smile.

"Well, congratulations on beating San Leandro. Please, go get something to eat."

"I'm fine for now, thanks," I said, holding my hand up. I marveled at how relaxed Pablo appeared. I knew that I'd be nervous in his position, especially since everyone expected Union City to win. Wasn't he afraid of looking bad in front of the huge crowd of supporters?

As Pablo left to joke with the many friends that he had in the crowd, I imagined a reporter coming up to me and asking, "Who would you rather face, Union City or Hayward?"

In professional sports, the coach or player always says something like, "It doesn't really matter. Both teams are going be tough."

In this case, I would be refreshingly honest. "Uh… duh! I hope and pray with all my heart that it's Hayward. We'd have a chance against Hayward."

So, I spent the next hour quietly rooting for Mean Gene's Hayward team. It was a difficult task, partly because I really disliked Gene and partly because Hayward was so overmatched. Gene and his partner, who had beaten Gary and me earlier this year with some creative line calls, were blown off the court 6-1, 6-2 by Union City's #1 doubles team. Union City's #2 doubles team looked equally impressive, winning 6-2, 6-0.

The large Union City crowd was loud, but polite. Using a steady diet of passing shots, Ming only prolonged the inevitable when he beat an aggressive Calvin 6-4, 6-3. Once Brian matched up against Hayward's #2 singles player, it was over, in a hurry, with Brian smacking baseline winners en route to an easy 6-1, 6-1 win. Union City had clinched the overall match.

I felt like one of those villains in the movies that sends out a hit man to knock off the powerful hero. Predictably, the hit man fails, his dead body delivered back to the villain. If anyone is going to take down Union City in our league, it would have to be us... next week.

On my way home, I received a cell phone call. I looked at the display and saw it was Stacey calling. I had not talked to her since our imposed "break", although we exchanged several emails. "Hi Stacey," I said, pulling over to the side of the road.

"Hi. I just wanted to say congratulations on your team's playoff win yesterday."

"Thanks. How'd you know?"

"I looked up the result on the internet. I know how important this was to you."

"It was," I said as there was a pause in the conversation. Stacey and I can usually talk for hours without taking a breath, but my mind was consumed with our situation. I wanted to tell her how much I missed her and that I loved her, but I also didn't want to send a mixed signal because I hadn't made up my mind on whether I could commit to an engagement and a promise to become a father.

"Well," Stacey finally said, interrupting the silence. "I just wanted to let you know I was thinking about you and wish you the best of luck in the league championship match."

"That's very nice of you." We briefly talked about some of the things going on with her before hanging up.

Pablo emailed me that the league championship match would be at noon on Sunday for the first three matches and then the final two would go on afterward. Even though he had plenty of courts, this is exactly what he did the week before in his playoff match against Hayward.

Faced with the toughest, most important match of the year, there are several strategies a captain can use to determine who plays. Who has played the best over the entire season? Who has been hot lately? Who plays the best in pressure situations? Who has had the most success against this opponent? I was forced to use the less successful strategy: Who's available, healthy and breathing?

Unfortunately, Gary had a family commitment that he could not break. Ross and Matt, who came up with the big win against San Leandro, both were unavailable, Ross with an ankle injury and Matt on his South American honeymoon. It was extremely frustrating that we would not be able to put our best team on the court in the league championship match.

On Thursday, I had dinner with Lloyd to talk about how we would line up. "It's not good," I said, slowly shaking my head. "I'm going to have to play with Craig and we'll have to promote Mike and Al, who were blown off the court the last time we played them. We're going to lose for sure."

"Don't say that," Lloyd said. "We just have to find a way to win three matches."

"They have two dominating doubles teams. We don't have a prayer to beat them."

Lloyd said with a shrug, "Then, we have to sweep the singles and win the remaining doubles."

"Last time we played them, their best player demolished Doc," I said, looking at the printout of the scores. "We'd have to line it up just right where Billy plays Brian and Doc matches up against this Calvin. Then, maybe, just maybe, we can sweep singles."

"Well, if Steve and I play the same doubles team as last time, which is their 3rd best, we can beat them."

"But, you'd have to be matched up against them, and there's only a 33% chance of that. And it's only a 50/50 chance that singles get matched up right."

Lloyd raised his eyebrows. "What would you say if I told you we could get the matchups we want at both singles and doubles?" Lloyd asked before explaining his plan.

On Sunday, Doc, Lloyd, Steve, Craig and I caravanned together, arriving a half hour before the start time. "Welcome back, my friend," Pablo said, greeting me with a smile. "Your team can warm up on this court." Many of the Union City players were already there, hitting ground strokes like 4.5 players on a nearby court.

The five of us warmed up on the court in front of the barbeque. When I sat down to take a break, I noticed it was 11:55 and looked around to find Pablo. Looking in my direction, Pablo appeared to be in deep thought. "Pablo!" I shouted. "We're ready. Are you ready to exchange lineups?"

"Just one minute, my friend," he said, walking back to the table to write something down. My heart beat rapidly as I hoped that Lloyd's plan would work. "Okay," Pablo said, waving me over.

I walked over to him and we exchanged lineup cards and I immediately smiled. Our plan worked perfectly.

"Wait a minute," Pablo said, dropping his tagline 'my friend'. "Some of these guys aren't here."

"They'll be here any minute," I said. "So, what court is each team playing on?" Shaken, Pablo pointed out the courts. "Okay, good luck," I said before walking a few steps away and calling Mike. He was waiting for my call a block away, sitting in a car with Mike, Al, and Billy. They had warmed up on a court a couple of miles away. "Okay, it worked. I need all of you here right away."

Our plan was to misrepresent who would be playing in the earlier round. Because Doc and Craig were present, Pablo put Brian at #1 singles. So, we got the matchup we wanted, having Billy play against Brian. This left Doc to battle the weaker Calvin. In doubles, by having Lloyd and Steve warm-up, we baited Pablo into playing both his strong doubles teams in the early round at #1 and #2 doubles. However, we played them at #3 doubles, matching them against their weakest team.

Within the next two minutes, the rest of the team arrived and everyone took the courts. Pablo, tight-lipped, had both arms crossed in front of his chest as I am sure he realized that he had been snookered.

When I saw the team Craig and I were matched up against at #1 doubles, I knew we were huge underdogs. I walked over to Craig and said, "We have absolutely nothing to lose playing these guys. Play loose and let's have some fun."

Craig nodded and we proceeded to play a strong first set. Did it matter? No. We were trounced 6-0 in the first set. Stretching to find a positive, we had several games go to deuce. They were the strongest doubles team that I had ever played, hitting winners from all over the court. Craig and I tried to adjust our game plan by poaching on our serve and varying our service return position on their serve, anything to try to get them out of their comfort zone. Nothing worked. Buoyed by a partisan crowd that cheered every one of their spectacular winners, we lost 6-0, 6-1.

Just as we were walking off the court, I saw Union City's #2 doubles team smash an overhead winner to close their match, blowing out Mike and Al 6-1, 6-1. Despite the fact we gave them little to cheer about, down 0-2, I admired the fact that we had a lot of Albany fans make the trip down. I was happy to see Doc's beautiful wife at the match in a front row seat. She was dressed in a revealing outfit that I could only hope would distract Doc's opponent. She gave Doc a kiss before he headed on the court.

Peter, who had been out with a knee injury all season, nonetheless made the trip to support the team. For the first time all year, Dale had come to our match. It meant so much to me that they traveled to see the match.

"How's Billy doing in his match?" I immediately asked Dale.

"He's down a set, but it's tied at two in the second set."

I exhaled audibly. The euphoria of lining up perfectly was gone. We lost the two matches we expected to, but that meant there was no margin for error. We couldn't lose another match or our season would be over. After Billy took the second set, all I wanted was for him to win to keep the overall match in doubt for the second set of matches.

Billy, considered a flake in past years and high maintenance at the beginning of this year, proved to be a great team player when it counted. He shifted his schedule to play in the playoffs last week and this week. Nearing the two hour mark in his match and drenched in sweat, Billy hit an overhead slam to break Brian's serve and take a 5-4 lead in the decisive third set. Laboring in the hot sun, Brian would alternate between holding both hands on his hips and knees in between points. Billy, sensing his opponent was weakening, took control of his service game, moving his exhausted opponent around the court to pull out the final set 6-4. This allowed us to close the gap in the overall match to 1-2 and every Albany fan greeted Billy with high fives.

I turned my attention to Steve and Lloyd, who had taken the first set 7-5. Steve, who had told me that he hadn't slept well all week after his loss against San Leandro, played an inspired match. He unleashed his power game with big forehands and big serves, punctuated with a few fist pumps. Lloyd was the consistent influence, both in his play and temperament. He made sure that Steve never got too high or too low. In the pressure-packed second set tiebreaker, Steve uncorked a power serve at match point. Union City's player sprawled out to barely return it and Lloyd put the soft return away with an angle volley. The overall match was now tied at two.

The entire contingent of fans, roughly 80 people, moved over to Doc's court to watch the deciding match. Doc had lost the first set 6-3, but led in the second set 5-4 with his opponent, Calvin, serving. Calvin, a serve and volley guy, was nullified by a passing shot at deuce point and then a perfect lob to take the set.

While the rest of our Albany group were cheering and giving each other high fives, Dale grabbed me by the arm. "I watched the last two games closely. Doc isn't foot faulting, but his opponent is, pretty badly. Doc has to be the one to call for a line judge, but when you talk to him, tell him to call for one during his opponent's first service game in the third set." Dale's savvy insight shocked me. I thought he was just enjoying the match, not analyzing details that could give us an edge.

I nodded before jogging onto the court to greet Doc. Lloyd, with two cold water bottles, followed behind me.

"Great job," Lloyd said to Doc as he handed him the bottles. "I think you can take him in this final set."

"I feel good," Doc said as he wiped sweat from his face with a small towel.

"Hey," I said, making sure I had his attention. In a lowered volume, I said, "Dale noticed that Calvin has been foot faulting. On his first service game, after a few points, tell him that you're noticing it and you're calling for a line judge."

I was worried that Doc might object, but instead he said, "Sounds like a good idea."

"Okay, great," I said before Lloyd and I left. After a five minute break, the third set started. Calvin broke Doc's serve to start the third set and I could feel a little air seeping out of the Albany crowd.

"I can't take this," I said. "I need to leave and do something less nerve-wracking, like defusing a bomb." I was nervous, but it helped to watch and joke with teammates in this tense situation. It was 30-all on Calvin's serve when Doc approached the net. I nudged Dale to make sure he knew what was happening. I couldn't hear most of the conversation, but I saw Calvin hold both arms out and say, "Whatever, man."

Doc walked over to the fence toward us. "We need line judges to call foot faults." There were some groans and a few heckles from the Union City crowd, but Doc did a great job of ignoring it.

Pablo and I selected representatives from each of our own teams. Al took the responsibility for us. He and one of the Union City players stationed on opposite sides of the net posts.

On Calvin's first serve, Al shouted, "Foot fault!" as he held up his arm. Calvin looked over at his representative who nodded. Mentally affected, Calvin proceeded to double fault and then netted his first volley to drop the game.

Doc had broken back and momentum had swung back in his favor. After Doc held serve, Calvin was called for another foot fault, this time by his own team representative. After that, Calvin started his serve three feet behind the baseline and began to double fault. Doc broke Calvin's serve and more importantly his concentration and focus. Up 3-1, Doc held serve at love to take a commanding 4-1 lead. I watched the match alongside Dale and Mike and we cheered for Doc on every point.

Doc saved his best tennis for the crucial sixth game when Calvin needed to hold. He smacked two crisp passing shots to break Calvin again and even the vocal Union City crowd went silent, possibly knowing the end was near. Doc went on to take the final set 6-2 and the entire Albany contingent raced out on the court to celebrate. One of the things I liked about this team is that it seems like it is a different hero every match.

Against all odds, we had toppled the mighty Union City in its own backyard and advanced to the District Championship. Amidst the celebration, Dale said to me, "Congratulations! It must feel great."

"Oh, it does. It does."

After receiving congratulations from Pablo, we went to a local pizza parlor to rejoice in our big triumph. For me, it was sweet victory, knowing all of the hard work, planning, and recruiting had paid off. I looked around the large table of diverse individuals and marveled how a group consisting of different races, generations, religions, professions, and economic backgrounds came together as a cohesive team. As we laughed and joked about the many memories of this year, I realized how enjoyable it was to have a team full of good friends.

"Hey, everyone!" Lloyd exclaimed with a mug of beer in his hand. "At the beginning of the season, a league championship for this team looked like a very long shot. Here's to Eric, who guided us through a miracle season."

"It was an Albany miracle!" someone shouted.

I had to fight back tears. It probably happened a long time ago, but this was the first time that I knew for sure that the players respected me as a captain and a leader. After the pizza party, I sat in my car alone in the parking lot, reflecting on the day's events. I pulled out my cell phone and instinctively started dialing Stacey's number to share this big moment. I paused after punching six of the seven numbers, realizing we were currently on a break. I cleared out the screen and instead dialed my parents.

My mom answered the phone. As soon as she recognized my voice, she said, "Hold on. Let me get your dad. He's been waiting to hear the news."

A few moments passed before my dad got on the line and said, "So, how did it go?"

"We did it. We beat Union City. We're going to Districts."

"Wow!" my dad said, sounding shocked.

My mom let out a cheer. "You must be so happy."

"I am."

"Well, I'm proud of you," my dad said. "Very proud. I know how hard you worked on this." I was speechless for a moment as I wiped a tear from my eye. Hearing my dad say he was proud of a tennis accomplishment meant the world to me. Noting the silence, my dad continued, "You captained a team to Districts in your first year. That's impressive."

I swallowed hard as I readied myself to make a suggestion. "Maybe you and Mom will be able to make it up to Districts."

"That's probably not a good idea," my dad said. "I'm not sure I could handle the stress of watching. But, we'll be there in spirit."

We talked for another few minutes before I hung up. As I sat in my car, I was a little disappointed that my dad wouldn't attend Districts. But, it was a fleeting thought. I was too happy with everything else to let anything get me down.

District Playoffs and Making the Big Decision

Out of the 253 teams that started, sixteen league champions advanced to the District Championships. At Districts, the sixteen teams are separated into four flights to play a round robin tournament where you play each team once. Late Monday night, four days before the big tournament, I was online, studying our three opponents. We play a Fresno team on Friday, San Francisco team on Saturday, and a San Jose team on Sunday.

My eyes bulged out as I looked on the San Francisco team's roster and saw Nate, our midseason castoff. Just when I thought I was done having to deal with him. We would face his team on Saturday and I'm sure Nate wouldn't miss that match for anything in the world. The undefeated San Jose team that we would face on Sunday was none other than the self-proclaimed "Dream Team" that told visiting teams they would not be providing food and drinks because they were saving their money for their trip to Nationals.

My phone rang and I answered it, immediately recognizing Stacey's voice.

"How have you been?" I asked. Over the last month, I had had a few conversations with her, but had not seen her since the imposed break.

"I'd like to get together and talk this week," Stacey said. "It's been a month."

"I want to get together too, but can we do it next week? I have Districts this weekend and we have practice several times this week." The phone went silent. "Stacey, are you there?"

"Yeah, you're doing it again. You're putting tennis ahead of our relationship."

"I'm not. It's just that this week is crazy. Next Wednesday, I'll come over to your house. Does that work?"

"Fine," Stacey said, seemingly still frustrated.

I cleared my throat before saying, "I want you to know that I've really missed being with you during the last four weeks."

There was an awkward silence as I waited for Stacey to say something... anything. She finally did. "Well, since you don't want to talk until Wednesday, there's really not much to say until then."

"I guess not," I said before we said our goodbyes.

Despite the obvious tension in my relationship with Stacey, I had to focus my attention on tennis. I did this during our last practice before Districts on Wednesday. After practice, I talked to my dad on the phone.

"What hotel are you staying at in Monterey?" my dad asked. "I'll want to be able to reach you if the results don't get posted soon enough."

"I'll be staying at the Hilton in Monterey, but your best bet is to reach me on my cell."

"Okay, I'll call you Friday night. And one more thing," my dad said, pausing to be dramatic. "Try to enjoy it, no matter what the result."

"I will. I promise."

When we met at the Albany courts to caravan down to Monterey on Friday, the team was at full strength. Ross had recovered from his ankle injury, Matt had returned from his honeymoon, and everyone successfully got off work on Friday, with Craig personally approving Billy missing a work day at the law firm. Also, Barry was back from his European vacation and he helped navigate on our drive to Monterey.

Leaving at 10:00 AM, we avoided the Friday morning traffic and made it to the outskirts of Monterey around 12:30. After stopping for lunch, Barry directed us to some practice courts where we spent 20 minutes loosening up.

Then, we drove to the Chamisal Tennis and Fitness Club in Monterey. Featuring 25 courts, a courtside café, and a clubhouse with a large screen television, it was an impressive venue. We followed the signs to the registration desk, located in a shaded kiosk.

 I turned in our lineup to a USTA official at the kiosk at 2:30 PM, thirty minutes before the scheduled start time. For the next half hour, we waited near the kiosk. Some guys were stretching while others watched District matches on nearby courts. I sat in a chair near the kiosk in the shade. I closed my eyes, remembered my dad's tapes, and meditated quietly. I had done everything I could to prepare myself and the team for this match. Just minutes before the match would be played, I wanted to rest my body and mind.

At 3:00 PM, they began calling players up. "Albany #1 singles, Doc and Fresno #1 singles, Denny, come up to the desk." I had done my research. Doc had drawn by far their best player. As 4.0 tournament player of the year, Denny had been featured in the Norcal section of the monthly *Tennis* magazine. In league play, he came into the match with an 11-0 record, a large improvement over last year. If you live in Fresno, I guess there isn't much to do other than work on your tennis game. In his late 20s, he casually walked up to the desk with a chorus of "You got 'em Denny. Take care of business."

I slapped Doc on the back as he headed to the court when a league official announced, "Albany #1 doubles, Eric and Gary. Fresno #1 doubles, Mario and Nicholas." Gary and I were matched up against two big, athletic guys in their 30s. We learned in warm-ups that our opponents were big hitters with their serves and groundstrokes. Our strategy was to get their serves back, get into a rally, and pick our spots to attack the net. We were rewarded when they would hit a groundstroke that flew over our heads, landing long. We won a hard fought first set 7-5 and had a 5-3 lead in the second set. Mario was serving to Gary, up 30-15, when he smacked a strong first serve to Gary's backhand. Gary's return hit the net and when I looked back, I saw him grimace.

He motioned for me to come over. With his back to our opponents, he said, "I just felt something pop in my elbow. It kills. I don't think I can play anymore."

I flashed back to Craig's injury and I wanted to handle this better. "What do you want to do?"

"I should get some ice on it. I could take an injury timeout, but I still don't think I'll be able to swing a racket. Your service game is coming up. I can stand on the edge of the court and you can try to play singles against them."

"I can't cover that much court, not against these hard hitters," I said before I got an idea. "Hey, I got it. Just go with me on this." I hustled back to my position as Gary looked confused. Mario's serve to me went out wide. I lunged for it, intentionally missing it and fell to the ground. I cried out and grabbed my ankle. Gary walked over to me with a smirk on his face. I called for an injury timeout and asked for two bags of ice. I hobbled over to the bench. When the ice arrived, I put one on my ankle and I handed the other to Gary. "Hold this one for a moment."

All eyes were on me and no one noticed Gary, who sat beside me, put the ice pack on top of a towel on his lap and rest his elbow on it. After about fifteen minutes, the official asked, "You need to make a decision. Are you going to retire?"

I slowly got up, faked my best limp and said, "I'll give it a try." It was my serve. As I walked to the baseline with Gary, I whispered to him, "All of the attention is on me. Just plant yourself on the net. They're going to go after me. If they hit it toward you, just let it go. No sense in you risking injuring yourself further."

The plan worked perfectly. Serving for the match at 5-4, all service returns came back to me. It was quite comical. I would race to get to a ball, but after getting to it and hitting a winner, I would limp back to the service line. I think they may have caught on to the ruse because at 40-30, Mario smacked his return right at Gary's head. Gary ducked and the ball sailed long. I jumped up and down a few times in celebration before I remembered I was supposed to have a bad ankle. I slowly limped toward the net to shake their hands.

After we got off the court, I learned that Denny, the star Fresno singles player, crushed Doc 6-1, 6-1, breaking his serve every time. We split the other two doubles matches with Ross and Matt winning while Lloyd and Steve fell to Fresno's best doubles team. So, it all came down to Billy, who had split his first two sets.

In Billy's match, it looked like a contest between David and Goliath as the Fresno player stood at about six foot five, nearly a foot taller than Billy. Members of both teams lined the hill overlooking the courts to watch the deciding match. At Districts, league officials require a 10 point tiebreak (first team to 10, leading by two) in lieu of a third set.

Billy played with determined confidence in the 10 point tiebreaker as he traded baseline groundstrokes that lasted at least twelve strokes. With the score tied at eight, things got very tense, especially for the large crowd. "Come on, Greg, you got this!" a member of the other team shouted.

Although excited, I watched with a level of calm that I never felt before, telling myself I was okay with any outcome. Nerves may have gotten the best of Billy as he double faulted to go down 8-9 and the serve switched to Greg.

Billy took a deep breath and readied himself to return serve. Greg uncorked a booming serve, which sent Billy sprawling, barely getting a racket on it. Billy's return was weak, meekly landing in the middle of the court. Greg moved a few steps in to make an easy put-away. I'm not sure if it was the pressure of the moment, but I could hardly believe it when he slammed the overhead into the top of the net. A gasp came over the crowd. Greg reacted instinctively, throwing his racket to the ground and swearing in frustration.

An official, watching just outside the court, raised his arm and announced, "Point penalty for the racket throw and point penalty for swearing."

A stunned Greg, with both hands on his hips, glared at his racket, which rested on the ground. He slowly picked it up before walking back toward the baseline, expecting to serve. When he turned around, he seemed confused to see Billy standing at the net. The agonizing truth soon dawned on him… the match was over! That miss had not only deprived him of a 10-8 victory, the two penalty points had turned a 9-9 score into an 11-9 victory for Billy. It was the strangest conclusion to a match I had ever seen. With subdued excitement, we all walked onto the court to congratulate the Kid on clinching our first District team win.

After the match, the whole team went out for dinner to celebrate. We all laughed as the team chastised me for my very fake limp on the court. Mike got up from his chair to do an impersonation of me. He hobbled around the restaurant, alternating every few seconds from limping to walking normally.

"Do you think they figured it out?" I asked over the laughter. Barry nodded as he smiled. "Oh yeah, by the end, they did." We also laughed about Billy's unbelievable "back-in" win and Doc's inability to hold serve once today. We were having so much fun it didn't bother me that it took so long for us to get our food. Doc finally complained about it, to which Mike said, "Well, if there's anyone who knows about bad service, it's you."

After dinner, I drove back to the Hilton, mentally and physically exhausted. Shortly after arriving at my room, I received a call from my dad. I told him the good news, but before I got too far into the story, he told me that he had to go and he would call me back soon at my hotel room. I gave him the room number and laid down on the bed. I took a deep breath, pausing to realize what an amazing day it was.

A few minutes later, I heard a knock at my door. I got up and opened the door, shocked to see my parents standing in the hallway.

They had driven 300 miles from Los Angeles to surprise me. I quickly hugged them and said how great it was for them to come.

After inviting them in, I asked my dad, "What about being with me just in spirit?"

My dad smiled. "Well, my body wanted to come along as well."

As I laid down to go to sleep for the night, I realized this was a perfect day… almost. The only thing that could have made it better was if Stacey was lying next to me.

I rode with my parents to the Chamisal courts the next morning as we faced off against Nate's San Francisco team, who lost yesterday to the "Dream Team" from San Jose. With

Gary's elbow still badly hurting, I had to shake up the doubles lineup, which now featured Lloyd and Steve, Mike and Al, and Ross and me. Although this was the first time I had played with Ross this year, we had been successful partners in previous seasons.

As I got out of the car, I felt a light wind. I zipped up my warm-up jacket, hoisted my tennis bag over my shoulder, and walked toward the facility. Despite the 9:00 AM start time, we had strong fan support. Even though they were not in the lineup, Craig and Chris had driven down to Monterey for Saturday and Sunday's match to support the team.

I sat down near the kiosk and waited to be called to the courts. I closed my eyes, cleared my mind, and let my body relax. Sometime later, I felt a hand on my shoulder. "If I didn't know any better, I would have thought you were meditating." It was my dad.

"Maybe a little," I said with a smile. "I'm guessing you approve."

"Maybe a little," he said with a smirk.

"Albany #1 doubles, Eric and Ross. San Francisco, #1 doubles, Nate and Damon!" shouted the USTA official behind the desk.

Hearing my name, I got up from my seat and walked a few steps to the front of the kiosk. It didn't fully sink in, though, that my former player Nate was my opponent until he joined me at the kiosk.

Nate, ignoring me, focused his attention on the USTA official. "You guys are on court #1, the stadium court. Right here," the USTA official said, pointing. "Good luck."

Nate took the balls from the official and headed to the courts.

"So, we drew Nate," Ross whispered as we followed behind Nate and his partner. "It's going to make our win that much sweeter."

When we got to our court, Nate's partner held out his hand and said, "I'm Damon." Ross and I shook his hand as we introduced ourselves.

Meanwhile, Nate was busy pulling out a bunch of rackets and setting them on the ground. He looked in our direction, lifted his head slightly, and said, "Hey, guys."

"Hi Nate," I said, raising my hand. I wasn't sure whether or not Nate was playing mind games by not shaking our hands. Many tennis players call this gamesmanship. I call it psychological warfare. I knew that I had to ignore him and concentrate on the match.

The first set was a very competitive one. From the very beginning, I could tell Nate was not treating this like any other match. He roared, "Yeah!" punctuated by an enthusiastic fist pump every time he hit a winner.

Despite Nate's distraction, Ross and I remained focused and won the first set. Midway through the second set, a strange thing happened. Nate not only was loudly cheering his winners, but our mistakes. There's an unwritten rule in tennis that you don't cheer your opponent's mistakes. At first, it was our ground stroke mistakes, then Nate celebrated our volley errors. He even started cheering our double faults, and believe it or not, he exclaimed, "Yes!" on one of our first serve faults.

His ridiculous antics were starting to get to us. It became a vicious cycle. He'd cheer our mistakes which made us angrier, causing us to make more mistakes. Nate was now even adding commentary like, "That's right. They can't handle the pressure. We got this."

"What a jerk," Ross said to me, serving down 2-4. "I'm blasting him."

I recognized that as tennis talk for trying to intimidate by hitting an opponent with a shot, even at the expense of losing a point. It's the tennis equivalent of throwing at a batter in baseball. "No," I said, shaking my head. "We can't afford it. Don't let him get in your head. Just play your game."

I'm not sure Ross ever really heard me. He was too upset with Nate's antics. On Ross' serve, Nate stood way up, nearly on the service line, in an obvious attempt to distract him. It worked. Ross double faulted and Nate put his hand up to his neck to show the choke sign. They had broken Ross' serve and his concentration. We were down 2-5.

During the changeover, I did my best to calm a seething Ross. Over the last few games, Nate's outbursts had drawn a small crowd to our court to see what was going on. Because of our proximity to the kiosk, many players from other teams were watching our match. Overwhelmingly, the crowd of strangers began to vocally support Ross and me.

This seemed to inspire us and we broke Damon, held my serve, and broke Nate to even the second set at five. At five all, Nate again stood on the service line and tapped his racket on the ground for an added distraction. Ross, remaining focused, hit two aces en route to holding serve to go up 6-5. I looked up at the crowd, which cheered loudly. My dad clapped enthusiastically and I felt a surge of adrenaline to close out the match.

Damon fell behind on his serve 15-40 and we had two match points. For the entire match, I had been returning cross court. Anticipating I'd do it again, Nate broke to the center of the court to poach my return, but I hit my return down the line to the empty alley for the game winner.

Ross and I screamed in exhilaration before we embraced. We walked to the net and shook Damon and Nate's hand. Nate gripped my hand tight and held it, forcing me to look him right in the eye.

"Congratulations. You guys played a great match. Good luck tomorrow." He released his grip and walked over to the sidelines.

I was stunned by his sportsmanship after showing none for the last two hours. I didn't have time to think about it further as the rest of my players mobbed Ross and me on the court. "You guys were the clinching match," Barry said to me. "We won the overall match 3-2."

My parents were at the end of the parade of people to congratulate me. My dad gave me a big hug and smile. He didn't need to say anything. The fact he was proud of me was written all over his face.

Before we left the Chamisal courts, we learned that San Jose's Dream team beat the Fresno club 4-1 to set up a showdown match tomorrow between us, with the winner advancing to the Sectional Championships.

That night, I met up with Lloyd and Barry at the hotel's bar to decide the lineup for tomorrow. We only had one disagreement: my suggestion to put Chris in the lineup to play with Ross.

"You spent the first part of the season trying to break them up as a doubles team," Barry said. "Now, you want to put them together in the most important match of the year?"

"Barry is right," Lloyd said. "I don't think Chris is ready. And this isn't the time to put someone in just to make them feel good."

"I'm not playing him as a favor," I said. "I think he's our best option."

"He's not ready," Lloyd repeated. "He's never played in anything other than a regular season match."

"He's never been given the opportunity to play in anything other than a regular season match. The last time he played, he and Ross won the match that put us in the playoffs. He's ready." I think the conviction in which I made my last statement stunned Lloyd and Barry. Both backed off, no longer contesting my decision.

As I walked back to my hotel room, I saw Doc and his wife in the hallway. When I began to remind Doc of the time that I wanted him at the courts tomorrow, his wife said, "I'll let you two talk logistics." She then turned to Doc, "I'll see you back in the room."

After Doc and I discussed timing, I asked him, "So, things are good with your wife?"

"Yes, they are."

"I've been talking about marriage with my girlfriend. It's nice to see examples of good marriages."

"I've been happily married for ten years," Doc said. "Hey, ten out of twenty-five ain't bad." Doc and I both laughed. "It's an old Dangerfield line."

"So, any advice to someone thinking about marriage?"

"Well, I recommend it if you're ready for it and it's with the right person. If so, it'll be the best move of your life. If not, it could be your worst."

"But, no pressure," I said with a chuckle.

"Look, I've watched you make all the right moves this season. If you apply the same good judgment about your relationship, you'll make the right decision."

When I woke up the next morning, I was physically and emotionally spent from the past two days at Districts. Despite my fatigue, it was easy to get psyched up to play today for the right to go to Sectionals.

When my parents and I arrived at the Chamisal courts, I noticed the San Jose team gathered near the kiosk. They were easy to spot since they all proudly wore white t-shirts with large, blue lettering spelling out, "The Dream Team."

After turning in our lineup, I noticed Chris sitting at a table by himself. "Nervous?" I asked, taking a seat next to him.

Chris tilted his head a bit before saying, "A little bit."

"Don't be. You get to play a doubles match at the District Championships with your best friend. Just focus on each point. Focus on the moment."

Chris nodded and then added, "Thanks."

"For what?"

"For everything. Sticking with me when I struggled earlier in the year. And now, giving me the opportunity to play."

I put my hand on his shoulder. "I didn't *give* you anything. You earned this opportunity. Enjoy it."

"Albany #1 doubles, Ross and Chris, San Jose #1 doubles, Scott and Dave!" a USTA official shouted.

"Okay, you're on," I said to Chris. "Go get 'em."

After Ross and Chris left the kiosk to go to their court, I took a quick look at the scorecard to see the names of our opponents. I walked back to a nearby table and pulled out my printout of their roster, which included city of residence and season record. Both of the guys I was matched up with were undefeated this year. Like many of their players, neither lived anywhere near San Jose, recruited from the far reaches of Northern California. I felt my blood pressure spike. I put the printout away, took a deep breath, and tried to relax.

Just as I closed my eyes, I heard, "Albany #2 doubles, Eric and Matt, San Jose #2 doubles, Jessie and Aaron."

I grabbed my bag and met Matt at the kiosk. "I'm Jessie," the behemoth of a man said as he reached the desk. Standing at least six foot four and well over two hundred pounds of mostly muscle, Jessie was an intimidating figure.

"You're on court five. Good luck," the USTA official told both teams. We shook hands with Jessie and his partner Aaron, who had a more mortal and less Herculean build. Because I struck up a conversation with Jessie, I actually walked with him to the courts.

"So, where do you live?" I asked, already knowing.

"Vallejo," Jessie said.

"Vallejo? That's pretty far from San Jose."

"Yep, almost two hours. Guys travel from all over to play on this team."

"Wow, but two hours..."

"It'll all be worth it when we make it to Nationals."

"Don't you mean *if*?"

"No," Jessie said, shaking his head. Jessie didn't speak in a condescending or arrogant manner. He said it as if he was stating a fact. The sky is blue, there are 50 states in the U.S. and we're going to Nationals.

I could feel my blood begin to boil. Now, not only did I want to make it to Sectionals, I wanted to be the team that stopped the Dream Team from making it.

As we began our five minute warm-up, I noticed Jessie hit with incredible pace and Aaron was very fleet of foot.

In the first game of the match, Jessie pounded two aces and two service winners. He not only hit with incredible power, but with perfect placement. I knew we had our work cut out for us.

After Matt held serve in a long game, we had the difficult task of trying to return Aaron's serve. Aaron hit his serve with incredible spin. Once the ball hit the ground, it spun in a completely different direction. It was the strangest serve I had ever seen. Once, I even swung and missed. The other times, Matt and I got to it, but hit an off balance shot that sailed out or was picked off at the net by Jessie.

We knew it was going to be a tough task to ever break either Jessie or Aaron. So, we would have to hold serve, which we did until I served, down 3-4. I was broken at 30-40 on a close line call.

Matt instinctively asked, "Are you sure?"

Of course, Jessie said, "Yeah." Jessie went on to close the first set with a strong service game.

"We've got to get more returns back off Jessie's serve," Matt said to me on the bench between sets.

"Well, let's give them a different look," I said. "I'm going to take a few steps back to give me a little more time to react. When they serve to me, you should take a few steps back as well to be in a better defensive position."

Our move to the baseline when returning serve helped, sort of. Now, instead of losing games at love, we lost them at 40-15 and 40-30. The good news is that we continued to hold serve and after eight games, we were tied at four.

At 30-40 in the 9th game, Matt served into Aaron's body. Aaron's backhand slice return hit the top of the net and dribbled over for a winner. It was a deflating moment for us. I could hear a collective groan from the Albany contingent in the crowd. Meanwhile, Jessie and Aaron, each with big smiles, excitedly gave each other high fives. They acted as if they had won the match. I guess they felt Jessie holding serve was a foregone conclusion.

"Okay, we have nothing to lose," I whispered to Matt. "The pressure is on them."

On the first point, Jessie smacked a serve out wide, which I lunged for hitting a lob toward Aaron. He leaped to execute a backhand cross court volley, but he hit it into the net. We were up love-15.

On the next point, Matt returned another blistering serve cross court. Jessie smacked a backhand just long. He stood flat footed, staring at our baseline indicating he couldn't believe our call. "They're tight," I said to Matt, ignoring Jessie.

After two service winners, Jessie double faulted to give us break point. After missing his first serve, Jessie hit a soft second serve. Matt ran around his backhand to smoke a forehand winner past a lunging Aaron. The crowd erupted with cheers while Jessie screamed in frustration and paced around the court with both hands on his hips.

The second set was now tied at five. Their large egos were beginning to take a hit and our confidence was on the rise.

Tennis is a game of momentum and we had it. I felt we could ride this wave to take the next two games for the set. But then, on the very first point of my serve, Jessie smacked a forehand return that hit the top of the net and dribbled over. Potentially still thinking about that bad break, I double faulted on the next point. Momentum had swung back in their favor. They went on to break my serve and win the match as Aaron held his serve.

The relief in their eyes as we shook our opponent's hands was only small consolation. The loss was a tough pill to swallow and it got even more difficult when I found out that we won two of the other three matches. So, we would have been going to Sectionals if we had won. Now, we had to hope Ross and Chris would pull out their match.

"They split sets and they're about to start a ten point tiebreak," Barry said. Other than Barry and my parents, everyone had already headed over to watch that deciding match.

"Tough match," my dad said, giving me a hug. "You really battled back in that second set."

When I saw my dad's smile, I was struck by a realization. He had the same proud, happy look as he did the day before when I won. Despite the sting of the loss, my dad's genuine reaction made me feel good. It's something that I kept on the forefront of my mind as I walked over to Ross and Chris' court.

When my parents and I arrived at their court, we joined a crowd of over 100 people. People were standing behind the courts on the hillside and all along one of the sides. The crowd consisted of players and family members from both teams and because the match decided the District Championship, I even noticed a few Fresno and San Francisco players. Ross and Chris' opponents were two average height, athletic guys in their 40s. From the score sheet, I remembered their names were Scott and Dave.

"What's the score?" I asked Billy, who had just loudly cheered a volley winner by Ross. "We're up 3-2 in the 10 point tiebreak."

"Their opponents are really tough, but Ross and Chris have been playing great," Craig said. As a first serve whistled by Ross, Craig winced. "My God, I can barely watch this."

"If you can't handle it, we'll just tell you what happens," Billy joked.

"No, it's like a horror movie," Craig replied. "It's scary, but you gotta see how it ends."

Somehow, some way, I was keeping my composure, even as everyone around me agonized on every point of the tiebreaker. It's not that I didn't care. Oh, did I care! I just reminded myself how far we had come as a team since we were mocked after our second match loss to a depleted San Leandro team and being blown off the court in our third match by Union City. It's like a poor man that wins the $3 million lottery and then becomes a finalist to win another million. I just wanted to enjoy this moment, surrounded by my teammates, who erupted when Chris hit a forehand winner that split his two opponents.

Things went back and forth in the tiebreaker. The score was tied at eight, both teams a mere two points away from becoming District champions. Ross served to Dave who hit a nice topspin lob that looked like a winner, but Chris, showcasing his athleticism, leaped up in the air and executed a perfect overhead slam in between his opponents. Chris pumped his fist in celebration, but didn't make a sound. Ross walked over to him to give him a high five and to talk strategy.

We were up 9-8, now only a single point away from advancing to Sectionals. It was the lefty Scott's serve. He hit a slicing serve out wide. Using a two handed backhand, Ross ran it down, but his return went into the top of the net. There was a collective groan that came from the crowd with the realization that the return was a couple of inches away from clearing the net. It was agony for the Albany contingent watching as Billy hopped up and down a few times in anguish and Craig dropped to one knee in frustration.

At 9 all, Scott hit his slicing serve down the middle of the court. Chris' backhand return was intercepted by Dave for a volley winner, giving the Dream Team a championship match point.

It's amazing how things can change in an instant in tennis. Moments ago, we were on the brink of an exhilarating victory, now on the edge of crushing defeat.

"Come on, Dream Team, bring it home!" Jessie bellowed. I'm not sure if it was appropriate for him to yell out like that before such an important point, but at six foot four, pure muscle, who's going to tell him to shut up?

Chris wiped his brow before readying himself to serve, down 9-10. He took a little off his first serve, perhaps to ensure he got it in. This allowed the lefty Scott to hit a hard low, crosscourt forehand return at the feet of a charging Chris, who hit a nice backhand cross court volley. Scott responded with another hard forehand groundstroke, this time toward Chris' forehand. Chris' forehand volley split his opponents, looking like a winner. But, just as I was about to celebrate, the ball sailed long.

Scott and Dave shouted in exhilaration and raised their hands in triumph. Our guys seemed stunned as the Dream Team players in the crowd flooded the courts.

"Hey, we gave them one heck of a scare. It was a great year," I said as I shook my teammates' hands in the crowd.

Then, I made my way to the court. I congratulated the Dream Team captain and their players. "Great job. Good luck at Sectionals."

"And Nationals," Jessie said to me.

Man, how I wished we would have beaten those guys. Still, I wanted to show good sportsmanship. So, I just smiled. As the

Dream Team contingent left the court, Billy and Craig were talking to Ross while Chris sat alone on the bench.

I sat down on the bench and before I could say a word, Chris spoke. "I'm sorry. I let you down," he said, looking off in the distance. "I let the team down."

"Hey, look at me," I said sternly. "You didn't let anyone down. I heard you played great all match. I saw you play great in the tiebreak. You battled out there, gave it your all and almost pulled it out. You made me proud out there." I slapped him on the back and whispered, "I know you're frustrated, but life is too short to be depressed. Take it as a learning experience. You'll pick yourself up, dust yourself off, and come back a better tennis player because of this experience."

Chris seemed speechless, merely nodding. Ross walked up to us, both hands on his hips. "So close, captain," Ross said, trying to crack a smile to conceal his disappointment.

"Hey, you guys were great," I said, giving Ross a high five. "The team did great. It was a great weekend, a great season."

Sectionals, Nationals and Life Lessons Learned

This chapter was supposed to detail our climactic win at Sectionals and our historic trip to Nationals. Unfortunately, fate had other ideas and our journey ended at Districts.

The day after our District loss, I felt in a daze with the finality of it all. The season was over. As content as I was with all of the accomplishments, I still felt a little depressed. A startling realization hit me. I wasn't really sad that we weren't going to Sectionals. I was simply sad that it was over. No more strategizing, no more practicing, no team lunches or parties, and no more league tennis matches for this unbelievable collection of players. The only tangible thing left from the season was a large banner the team put up on our home courts, titled the "Albany Miracle". Below that, it stated "4.0 East Bay Champions" and the year.

Sure, you can say, "There's always next year." But, in USTA league tennis, that's not necessarily true. It's doubtful we'll ever have the same collection of players again. Some will move up to the 4.5 level and some will not. Others might move out of the area or decide to take a year off league tennis.

I really was more disappointed that our season had come to the end than missing out on some mystical trip to Nationals, which proves the old adage, "It's the journey, not the destination." That's the secret to life: enjoying the journey. Imagine a train passenger staring at his watch counting the seconds until he reaches his destination. Meanwhile, he misses the amazing views of the changing scenery outside his window. Instead of stressing about the outcome of tight matches, I should have been enjoying the bonding experience of going through this incredible season.

Life is about making meaningful connections with other people. The ability to have as many great memories as you can, and actually enjoy them as they happen, separates the happy people from the less happy. When I look back on this season, I'll remember the team camaraderie. I'll remember how I started rooting against one of my doubles teams and ended putting them together in the biggest match of the year. To sum it up, I'll remember the pizza parties and the joking at practices more than any specific shot that I may have hit on the court.

In life, you can achieve many things as an individual. You can graduate from college or get a promotion at work, but I think successes like the ones our team achieved are more special because you achieved that goal by working as a part of a group. As a team, we have shared the same trials and tribulations, which creates a special bond. This bond makes me think of my teammates as a band of brothers.

Life has a way of making you constantly desire more. You spend your life wanting to just make a $100,000 annual salary, then if you're lucky enough to attain that, you want to make $150,000. A general economic paradox is the more money you make, the more money you feel you need. In tennis, I just wanted to make the playoffs, then I just wanted to win our league, and then when we made Districts, I wanted to make it to Sectionals. The thing about USTA leagues is that there is only one national champion. Every one of the approximately 4,000 other teams end their season with some disappointment that they did not go further.

Why as human beings can't we be satisfied with what we have? Why are we always in the pursuit of happiness? What if we are already happy? Sometimes, society dictates our perception of happiness. We aren't making enough money or we aren't driving a nice enough car. Perhaps we aren't winning enough league tennis matches or we aren't winning convincingly enough. Eventually, we'll feel pressure to start trying to win at love in each game.

When trying to maximize my happiness, I try not to look to others. It's like my dad has always told me, "Don't let others define your success." Well, others shouldn't define your happiness either.

Society dictates that life follows a specific script. In the last two years of high school, everyone asks, "What college will you attend?" Then, they want to know your major followed by what job you're going to land after college. Then, in relationships, people want to know when you're dating, then when you're dating exclusively, and then when you're getting married before finally, when you are going to have children. All the while the questioner assumes you want to take the next step.

As I drove to Stacey's house Wednesday evening, I thought about how happy I was exclusively dating her. Why did we have to mess with that? Would our relationship be better in marriage? Would it be enhanced with children? The truth is I enjoyed some independence. I have to admit that there are times when I enjoy a short break apart from Stacey. But, this last month taught me one thing. I didn't enjoy a long break. I missed being with her terribly.

When I arrived, I greeted her with a hug and a kiss. She smiled with a sparkle in her eye, apparently happy to see me.

She invited me in and we sat down on the sofa in her living room. I immediately said, "Here's what I know. The nearly three years that we have been dating have been... just outstanding. The last month without you has not." I grabbed her hand and said, "I love you so much. I know you want to get married and I don't want to lose you, so let's do it. Let's get married."

Stacey's facial expression changed. She let go of my hand and glared at me. It wasn't the reaction I expected.

"What?" I asked.

"You had a month to think about it and that's what you come up with. You'll get married because *I* want to. Just answer this. Do you want to get married to me? And I need you to be 100% honest."

"Honestly, yes," I said, looking at Stacey. "You gave the ultimatum. Either we marry or we break up. I definitely opt to get married."

Stacey looked at me as if I was a hostile witness in one of her court cases. "I need another honest answer. Do you want to have children?"

I took a deep breath and exhaled audibly, all the while maintaining eye contact with Stacey. "Yes, because you want to..."

"Forget about me," she snapped. She peered at me with squinted eyes. She waved her hand in the air and said, "Assume I'm ambivalent. Would you want to be a father?"

"Right now, no," I said. Stacey fell back against the sofa cushion. I quickly added, "That was just answering for myself. If you really want to have kids, I'm willing to do it."

"Listen to yourself. You're *willing* to have kids, like it's a favor to me."

"What do you want from me?" I asked, growing frustrated.

"I don't know," Stacey said, sounding exasperated before pausing to look up at the ceiling. She looked back at me. "I just hoped you'd love to be the father of our kids. It just isn't very romantic if you treat it like a sacrifice. Well, you don't have to worry. I've given it a lot of thought and I don't want us to have kids."

"You don't?" I said with a smile.

Stacey stared at me. Her eyes began to well up. Confused and speechless, I stared back, feeling a lump in my throat. "You were smiling," Stacey said, holding her hand over her chest. She shook her head. "You couldn't be happier with the thought of not having kids."

"Hold on," I said, still confused. "You just said that you didn't want to have kids. It seems we agree…"

"That's not what I said. I said I don't want *us* to have kids. My children deserve a father who wants to be a father. And that's not you. Your smile reveals the truth. You don't want to have kids and you don't really want to get married. You just want to date. I've put my personal life on the back burner in favor of a career. Not anymore. I want to get married and I want children. You've had three years to get to the place where I am and you aren't even close." Her lips quivered as she paused for a moment. "I think we should break up."

"Break up? What are you talking about? I told you that I will get married and we can have a child, if that's your dream."

"My dream is to have a child with someone who wants a child."

"Well, maybe I don't, but the fact that I will do it anyway should show you how much I love you. It should show you how devoted I am."

"You know me," Stacey said, tilting her head. "I always want the best for myself. I deserve it, and so does my family. I deserve a man who wants to be my husband and my kids deserve a father who wants to be their parent."

I groaned as I buried my face in my hands. It was an excruciatingly difficult conversation. We continued to talk for the next two and a half hours, but it felt like we were just going around and around in circles basically repeating the same points. Emotions ran high. There were raised voices, frustrated groans, and emotional tears. But, after it all, the conclusion was that Stacey wanted to end our relationship.

"My mistake was trying to change you," Stacey said, sniffling. "My mom always told me that you should never try to change a man unless he's in diapers." Stacey forced a smile, but I didn't laugh. I was far too depressed. "The bottom line is," Stacey said, her smile gone. "If you don't really want to be a parent, for yourself, then there's no sense in trying to make you become one."

The next week and a half was very difficult. I had a hard time focusing during the day and a hard time sleeping at night. I missed Stacey tremendously. I wanted to call her several times, but I had no idea what to say.

Nothing seemed to make me feel better: not talking to my parents, not eating my favorite foods, and not even hanging out with my friends. Other than work, I began to cut myself off from the outside world. On Sunday afternoon, I was still depressed, unable to laugh once during a television sitcom.

Bored, I shut the television off and checked the USTA website to look at the Sectional results. I was surprised to see a Fremont team had won all three matches, including beating San Jose's Dream Team 4-1. So, it turns out that Jessie and his team of hired guns would not be going to Nationals after all. I have to admit a smile curled across my lips for the first time in the last ten days, but it only lasted a few seconds.

I turned the computer off and pulled out my blood pressure kit and tested myself. After the air pressure was released, a reading of 122 over 80 showed on the display. I noted it in my record keeping. That's twenty straight normal blood pressure readings. With medication, diet and regular exercise, I had kept my blood pressure under control. I was happy with the results, but it did little to change my current depressed state. I wrote myself a note to call my doctor to see if I could be weaned off medication.

As I stared out the window, I began to think how playing league tennis is similar to intimate relationships. In both, you put yourself out there for everyone to see. Then, you become emotionally invested in the results. When things go well, there's no greater feeling in the world. But, when things go wrong... really wrong, it hits you at the core, making you ponder getting out of "the game" forever. I worried about my future... would I ever find anyone who I loved like Stacey? Now, nearing my 37th birthday, was I destined to grow old without a significant other whom I truly loved?

My phone rang, interrupting my sad thoughts. I had been letting the answering machine get it, but for some reason I decided to pick up.

Hello.

Hi Eric. It's Chris from tennis. How's it going?

Honestly, not too well. But, I'd rather not talk about it. It's kind of a long story.

Oh, sorry. I just called to thank you for everything: giving me a chance to play on the team, working with me, believing in me, and most of all, the support you gave me after the matches.

Of course, Chris. We're teammates.

Well, I really appreciate all of the advice, especially helping me mentally.

Really? What helped you the most?

When you told me to live in the moment. Don't worry about the past and don't concern yourself with what lies ahead in the future. Focus on the moment, focus on execution, and enjoy the moment.

Wow, that's good advice.

Yep, and you said life is too short to get upset or depressed when you have a setback. A setback is just a learning opportunity. I was too depressed to remember that right after the District match, but it's like you said, you have to pick yourself up, dust yourself off, and come back stronger next time. [There was a profound silence on the line]. *Look, I didn't mean to take too much of your time. I just wanted to say thank you. Sorry you're not feeling well.*

Actually, I feel better. I really do. Thanks to you.

Me? What did I do?

You reminded me not to be obsessed with the regrets of yesterday and the fear of tomorrow, but instead, to simply enjoy today.

Hmm… speaking of today, do you want to hit the tennis ball later?

Yeah, I'd like that. I'd like that very much.

Other novels by this author:

TRYING TO WIN
AT LOVE AGAIN

A FINAL JOURNEY THROUGH
AN EXTRAORDINARY
USTA TENNIS SEASON

ERIC LEE

In this humorous and inspiring sequel to the novel you just read, *Trying to Win at Love*, the narrator loses his championship-winning team and long time girlfriend. Faced with new challenges, he discovers that old approaches don't always provide the solution. Without the comfort and familiarity of the past, he struggles in his attempt to find a new team and mend a broken heart. In the process, he learns a lot about himself and life as he once again tries to win at love.

For more information about the author and his stories, please visit his official website at www.ericleestories.com.

Other short story collections by this author:

This book features ten short mystery and suspense stories sure to entertain, surprise, and intrigue the reader. In one of the short stories, a young accountant is working late in the office. Living alone, he calls home to leave himself a reminder message. Instead of hearing his answering machine, someone answers the phone. When he asks to speak to himself, the familiar voice says, "Speaking". He quickly comes to a startling realization. The voice sounds identical to his.

This book features nine short mystery and suspense stories. In the short story, *Murder in a Coastal Town*, a homicide detective, is overcome with grief at the murder of his eight-year-old son. The only witness to the murder is his eleven-year-old daughter. How does he extract detailed information about the murder from a witness who is desperately trying to forget? Will the detective ever be able to catch the murderer and what emotional price is he willing to pay?

This book features nine short mystery and suspense stories. In the short story, *Murder in a Snow Covered Town*, a beautiful ten-year-old girl has disappeared. Her grief-stricken parents, frustrated with the progress of the police, enlist the help of private eye Robert Douglas to find her. Has she been taken or did she merely run away? Will the police or will the detective find her first? And will she be found dead or alive?

For more information about the author and his stories, please visit his official website at www.ericleestories.com

www.ingramcontent.com/pod-product-compliance
Lightning Source LLC
Chambersburg PA
CBHW071309130626
46556CB00004B/1539